She longed to tell him "Dale was never my lover!"

Like someone trapped in a dream, Sarah watched Ben emerge from the water. Her eyes followed his progress, noting the tautly sleek and tanned skin that sheathed his muscles, his indifference to his nudity....

Suddenly the dream spell broke and the pounding of the surf was echoed by the heavy thud of her own heart. Panicked, she began to run blindly, not knowing why she was running or where, propelled by some nameless instinct. She could hear him behind her; she could almost feel the heat of his breath against her skin, but still she ran, her feet slowed by the gritty silk of the sand. Then Ben's arms reached out to grab her, the impact of his body driving out her breath, and she fell helplessly onto the sand, taking Ben with her....

Books by Penny Jordan

PENNY JORDAN

shadow marriage

Harlequin Books

TORONTO • NEW YORK • LONDON
AMSTERDAM • PARIS • SYDNEY • HAMBURG
STOCKHOLM • ATHENS • TOKYO • MILAN

Harlequin Presents first edition July 1984
ISBN 0-373-10706-4

Original hardcover edition published in 1984
by Mills & Boon Limited

CHAPTER ONE

'SARAH?'

She recognised the voice of her agent immediately, and her fingers tensed on the receiver in response to its jovial tone, hope feathering fingers of tension along her spine.

'Good news,' Carew told her buoyantly, 'and not ad-work this time, before you ask. It's a film part, and a good one. Want to hear more?'

The teasing enquiry reminded her that she was twenty-three and not eighteen, and long past the stage of dry-mouthed excitement over any part.

'It depends,' she responded cautiously. Her voice was warmly husky; extraordinarily sexy, was how one director had once described it, but Sarah had made it clear to Carew before she became one of his clients that she had no intention of accepting parts that emphasised or relied on her sexuality—in any way. And she had stuck to her statement rigidly, even though it had often meant that she had been forced, on more than one occasion, to take other jobs to pay her rent—working in shops and offices, glad of the odd well paid commercial which came her way.

'It's a beaut,' Carew assured her, and although she could not see his face she could picture it well enough, and the jumbled chaos that passed for his office.

'You'll love it,' he continued. 'I'm having the

script sent round to you right away. We've got a meeting with the director tomorrow. Lunch at the Savoy. You're one lucky female, Sarah. The part was as good as cast, and then Guy Holland happened to see that ad you did for the shampoo people. You'll be flattered to know that he rang me at home last night. It's only by chance that he's over here at all. A large part of the filming is going to take place in Spain. He's a stickler for authenticity, and he was only in London overnight, so . . .'

'Carew, tell me more about the film,' Sarah cut in quickly. She knew Guy Holland's reputation— who didn't in the film world?—and there was only one other director that she could think of who possessed an equivalent aura; whose name provoked the same powerful charisma.

'Oh, it's about Richard the First,' Carew told her obligingly, 'and before you ask, it's no mere costume piece. According to Guy the screenplay is one of the best he's ever seen, and it's been written by an amateur, someone who has guarded his identity so closely that no one seems to know exactly who he is. Anyway,' he seemed to collect his thoughts with an effort, as though he realised how tense and impatient she was growing, 'it seems the long and short of it is that Guy wants you to play Joanna—Richard's sister. The part's a gem, Sarah. I've only glanced through the screenplay, but what I've read is enough to convince me that Guy isn't exaggerating when he says he's got half a dozen top actresses going down on their knees for it.'

'But his budget is limited, and so he's got to make do with me,' she cut in drily.

'No way. Like I told you, Guy is a stickler for accuracy, and according to him your colouring is exactly right for Joanna. The first thing he wanted to know was if your hair was natural.'

Sarah pulled a wry face into the receiver. Her hair was a particularly distinctive red-gold, and she had the pale Celtic skin to go with it— unfashionably pale really, her eyes a deep smoky grey, bordering on lavender whenever her emotions were intensely aroused.

'The second thing he wanted to know was how long it was. It's just as well you didn't agree to have it cut for that ad. Apparently whoever plays Joanna must have long hair.'

Sarah grinned to herself as she listened to him. At the time he had been all for her having her hair cut as the shampoo company had wished, but she had been with Carew long enough to accept that at bottom his clients' interests were paramount.

'Excited?' he questioned.

'I might be—when I've read the part.'

She didn't say any more, but he interpreted her remark easily.

'It's perfectly all right—there aren't any sex scenes. At least, not for you. I've already checked that out. The script should be with you within the hour. Give me a ring when you've read it, won't you?'

As she replaced the receiver Sarah tried not to give in to the insidious tug of excitement spiralling through her. A film part as juicy as this one promised to be was a gift she had long ago made up her mind she would never receive. For one thing, she liked living and working in London,

which was hardly the Mecca of the film world. For
another, her insistence on parts without any sexual
overtones automatically narrowed her field considerably. She knew quite well that Carew was
curious about her rigid refusal, his instinct telling
him that there was more to it than a natural
disinclination to use her body to further her
career. After all, she had joined him straight from
her part in the highly acclaimed film of
Shakespeare's life in which she had played the
wanton Mistress Mary Fitton of Gawsworth—
Shakespeare's 'Dark Lady'.

For that part she had received rave reviews. She
had put her heart and soul into it, immersing
herself completely in it, so much so that afterwards
she had wondered if she hadn't been infected with
some of Mary's wantonness herself. Certainly that
would explain why she had . . .

The heavy clatter of something falling through
her letter box dragged her thoughts away from the
past, and she hurried into the small hall, picking
up the heavy package, and retreating with it to the
comfort of her sitting room.

Her flat might only be small, but Sarah had an
inborn flair for colour and tranquillity—something
she had inherited from her parents, no doubt. Her
father had been an acclaimed interior designer,
and her mother his assistant. The one shred of
comfort she had been able to salvage from the
destruction of her life after they had been killed in
a plane crash had been that they had gone
together.

She had only just entered drama school when it
happened; a late entrant, having decided at the last

minute not to go on to university, but to try her hand as an actress instead.

She had only been nineteen when she was offered the part of Mary Fitton. Shakespeare had been played by Dale Hammond, an actor whose star was very much in the ascendant. Unlike her, Dale had gone on to international fame, and a smile plucked at Sarah's lips as she remembered several instances of his Puckish sense of humour. They had got on well together, so well that she had found no embarrassment in their intensely emotional and sensual scenes together, unlike those she had had to play with Benedict de l'Isle, the actor who was playing the Earl of Southampton, her other lover, and reputedly Shakespeare's as well!

As she unwrapped the package, she shivered, suddenly cold, unwilling to remember the desire that had flamed between the two of them; a desire which had left its mark on the film, highlighting the emotional drama they played out as Southampton and Mary Fitton. Dale had been her friend, and in consequence of their friendship she had been able to relax while they played their love scenes, but with Benedict there had been no relaxation possible. And that was why . . .

The script slipped from her fingers, landing on the polished wooden floor with a thud, bringing her sharply back from the past. Schooling her thoughts, Sarah bent and picked it up, flicking through the opening pages and then going back to read them more slowly as the typed words enthralled her imagination.

Two hours later, when she put aside the final page, her thoughts were still coloured by all that

she had read. For that brief span of time she had
been living in the twelfth century, totally absorbed
by the lives of the characters she had been reading
about; Richard, third son of Henry II and his
estranged wife Eleanor of Aquitaine; adored by his
mother and hated by his father. Richard, who
would one day be king. Sarah shivered in sudden
reaction, trying to visualise the man who had
written so sensitively and deeply about a man who,
she realised for the first time, had been an
intensely tortured individual, torn between duty
and desire, unable to fulfil one without destroying
the other. She didn't have enough knowledge
about the Plantagenet era to know how factual or
otherwise the script was, but she remembered
enough to sense that it had been carefully
researched, and that in depicting Richard as a man
tormented by his intense love for another knight,
the writer had leaned towards the truth rather than
inventing the relationship simply for effect. Having
read the script, it was dizzyingly heady to know
that Guy Holland wanted her for Joanna. The part
wasn't a large one, but then none of the female
parts were. The only other ones of any magnitude
were Eleanor, Richard's mother, and Berengaria,
his wife.

Unlike earlier thirties films about Richard, this
one was not concerned primarily with the Third
Crusade, which she was surprised to see had
occupied a relatively short span of Richard's life.
What did amaze her was the discovery that he had
first gone to war as a teenager, defying, and
eventually defeating, his father. But it was her part
as Joanna she must concentrate on. She had three

major scenes—the first when Richard accompanied
her through Spain on her way to her first husband,
the aged William of Sicily, a man who was fifty to
her seventeen; the second when Richard came to
Sicily with his army en route for the Crusade and
rescued her from her unscrupulous brother-in-law,
Tancred, following the death of William, and the
third when she renounced the man she loved—one
of Richard's knights—before agreeing to marry
Raymond of Toulouse, her second husband.

Carew hadn't exaggerated when he described the
part as 'meaty', and Sarah hurried to the phone,
quickly dialling his number.

Heather, his assistant, recognised her voice
straightaway and put her through.

'Umm, that voice—it's like being drowned in
melted honey!' Carew told her extravagantly. 'Guy
will find it a bonus he hadn't expected. Well,
you've read it, I take it? What do you think?'

'You know what I think,' Sarah managed in a
husky whisper. 'Oh, Carew . . .'

Stupidly tears filled her eyes and she had to
shake them away. She had fought so hard to tell
herself that it didn't matter that her career had
never been the success she had wanted, that she
had hardly dared to let herself hope that she might
get a part like this. Now she no longer doubted
that Guy Holland hadn't been boasting when he
claimed that half a dozen Hollywood greats were
clamouring for it, and she could only bless the
perverseness that made him such a stickler for
detail that he wanted a genuine long-haired
redhead for his Joanna.

'Well, don't forget there's still tomorrow,'

Carew cautioned her, quickly soothing her leaping fears by adding, 'Not that you've anything to worry about. Once Guy sees you . . .'

'Who's playing Richard?' Sara wanted to know.

'An old friend of yours.' He paused expectantly, and Sarah felt her blood run cold. 'Dale Hammond,' Carew told her, obviously disappointed by her lack of response. 'Apparently Guy has certain reservations about him, but his colouring is right, and there's no denying that he has the experience for the part. Guy is very anxious that Richard should be played sympathetically, and yet remain very much the male animal.'

The part would be extremely challenging and taxing, Sarah could see that, and in her mind's eye she collated Dale's roles since his *Shakespeare*. He had the experience for the role, he also had the slightly malicious sense of humour that had come across so well in his *Shakespeare*, and which was evident in some ways in *Richard*, but he would need intense depth and breadth for the role, if he was to be played as she sensed the playwright had intended him to be. As she hung up, promising Carew that she would not forget their lunch date, she frowned thoughtfully, curious about the writer of the film, experiencing something which was almost a comradeship with him, so caught up in the spell of his words that it was almost as though her senses knew him.

She spent the morning in her local library, and emerged with her arms piled high with reference

books, with barely an hour to spare before her
lunch date.

She dressed quickly; a dove-grey silk dress with
undertones of lavender to darken her eyes, leaving
her skin free of make-up apart from a slick of
colour along her lips, braiding her hair and
twisting it into a coronet on top of her head.

The effect was startling, and she smiled a trifle
wryly at her haunting reflection. Guy Holland was
no fool. He would realise instantly that she was
trying to portray his 'Joanna'. Whether she had
succeeded or not she had yet to discover.

She arrived exactly on the dot of one and was
shown to a secluded table in the cocktail bar.
Carew's eyes widened as he saw her and he
struggled to his feet, a small, rotund man, with a
shock of untidy fair hair and owlish brown eyes.
His companion uncoiled himself from his chair far
more elegantly, one lean, tanned hand extended to
grip hers, his eyes coolly appreciative as they
studied her, and was studied in return.

His first question wasn't what she had expected
at all. His glance lingered on her hand as his own
was withdrawn, and she had to fight against a
deeply instinctive desire to wrench off the plain
gold ring adorning her left hand.

'You're married?'

'I ... I'm divorced,' she managed curtly,
frowning as Carew rushed into what she considered
to be unnecessary explanations. 'Sarah was
married briefly to Benedict de l'Isle.'

'Really?' Darkly silvered eyebrows rose speculatively. 'I know Ben quite well. I hadn't realised
he'd been married.'

'I'm sure he wants to forget it as much as I do,' Sarah told him, glaring at Carew. What on earth had he said anything for? He knew she abhorred all mention of her brief and all too disastrous marriage to Benedict de l'Isle. A marriage that had been over almost before it had begun. A marriage entered into through ignorance and folly on her part and reluctance and guilt on Benedict's. How much reluctance she had discovered on the night of their wedding. Thank God Dale had been there to help her. Without him . . .

'You've read the script. What do you think of it?' Guy asked her, resuming his seat.

'It's marvellous.' Her eyes glowed with conviction. 'The whole thing's so powerfully compulsive that I feel I almost know the writer. He makes you feel what's written; experience Richard's anguish, and understand all that he must endure. I . . .' She broke off, feeling flustered as she realised Guy was watching her speculatively. 'I'm sorry,' she apologised awkwardly. 'You must be used to this reaction by now.'

'I'm certainly used to hearing the script praised,' he agreed, 'but you're the first person I've come across to mention the actual writer with such emotion. Normally any emotion is reserved for the box office receipts, or star prestige,' he added with dry cynicism. 'You feel you could handle the part?' He watched her carefully as he spoke, and Sarah sensed that his question was in some way a test.

'I hope so. Joanna grows from a child to a woman during the course of the film. She falls in love with Richard's squire as a child, but gives herself to him as a woman, knowing the price she must pay for her love is marriage to Raymond of Toulouse.'

'I hear you flatly refuse to play any heavy sex scenes,' Guy intervened, suddenly changing the subject. 'Why?'

Sarah shrugged, her palms damp, fear cramping through her although she fought to control it. 'Perhaps because I feel true sensuality is more effective for being implied than actually witnessed.'

'Umm. I suspect the two actors who are to play Richard and his lover heartily feel the same thing. Unfortunately, as far as they are concerned the script calls for some decidedly physical scenes.'

'Oh, but in the context of the script they're . . .' She broke off, flushed and confused, as Guy Holland turned to her.

'Go on,' he prompted, 'they're what?'

'Almost hauntingly emotional,' she responded hesitantly, unable to find the words to convey the terrible sadness that had gripped her when she read the script.

'Let's just hope the censors see it that way,' Guy told her with another flash of dry humour.

They were shown into the restaurant and were halfway through their meal before he put Sarah out of her misery and confirmed that she had got the part.

'You won't be an entirely popular choice,' he warned her, 'but as far as I'm concerned, you're the right one.' He went on to discuss other members of the cast. Berengaria was to be played by a well known film star whose smoulderingly sensual nature was at such odds with Berengaria's naïve innocence that Sarah could only hope that she was an excellent actress.

'She wasn't my choice,' Guy told her, startling her by reading her thoughts, 'but let's just say she comes with the script, and I wanted it badly enough to agree.'

Sarah caught her breath. Did that mean that Gina Frey knew who had written the screenplay and was romantically involved with him?

It was a question she sensed would not be answered even if she asked, so instead she opened a discussion about filming sequence and dates and discovered that most of the filming was to be done in Spain, where there were enough castles, desert and empty spaces for them to be able to recreate the feel of the twelfth century.

After lunch they returned to Carew's office to finalise details and sign contracts, promising that she would be in Spain for the end of the month.

'After all,' she commented to Carew when Guy had gone, 'what's to stop me?'

'You'd better go out and buy yourself a ton of sunscreen,' Carew warned her. 'Guy won't be too happy if your skin gets burned, and you'll be filming all through the summer. I wonder why he wanted to know about your marriage?' he added, eyeing her thoughtfully. Although he was basically a kind-hearted man, on occasions it irked him that Sarah was so resolute about not discussing her brief marriage. After all, Benedict de l'Isle was of sufficient importance in the film world for his name to carry weight; Sarah could have used it. When she had first come to him he had read up on her press-cuttings, and it had been from them and not from her that he had learned of their affair while they were playing opposite one another in *Shakespeare*; she as Mary Fitton and he as Southampton, the man who ultimately destroyed her. They had been married at the end of the filming; there had been a party for all the cast, and then, within a week, it was all over. To quote Benedict de l'Isle, as many of the papers had done with evident glee, his new wife, like Mistress Fitton, had been unable to choose between her two lovers and in the end had chosen wrongly. He eyed Sarah obliquely. If de l'Isle had been speaking the truth, did that mean that she and Dale had been lovers, and if so . . .

Anxious to get back to her library books and her research, Sarah was oblivious to his thoughts. This part was a gift from the gods in more senses than one. Another twelve months without a decent part and who knows, she might have been on the verge of abandoning her career. But she *had* got the part, and she fully intended to leave her stamp on it; to *be* the Princess Joanna, spoiled darling of the greatest house in Christendom until the woman accepted what the child could not; that princesses were but pawns, bought and sold to bind allegiances.

CHAPTER TWO

THERE would be a car waiting for her at the airport, Guy had promised, and Sarah looked dazedly for it as she emerged from the terminal building, and into the slumbrous heat of the Spanish night.

Because it was the height of the tourist season, she had had some problems getting a flight and, in the end, had had to fly in on a late evening one. She was a relative newcomer to the cast, and she knew from what Guy had told her that some studio filming had already taken place, mainly the earlier scenes involving Richard as a youth and some of his clashes with his father. Telling herself that it was only natural that she should feel nervous, she searched the row of stationary cars, wondering which one was waiting for *her*.

'Sarah! Sweetling!'

Even if she hadn't recognised the tall, broad-shouldered man striding towards her, she would have recognised the endearment he had picked up when they filmed *Shakespeare*, and his name left her lips on a pleased cry as she hurried towards him.

'Dale, put me down!' she protested as he swung her up into his arms, kissing her theatrically, adding with a grin, 'I'm honoured, aren't I, dear brother? Being collected by my liege lord himself, and the most prominent member of the cast.'

'And I haven't come alone,' Dale told her,

moving slightly aside so that Sarah could see the man standing behind him. Tall with brown hair, he smiled warmly at her, his brown eyes faintly amused by Dale's obvious 'play-acting'. 'Meet your lover-to-be,' Dale told her, adding, 'Paul, come over here and be introduced to Sarah.'

As they shook hands, Sarah found herself warming to Paul with a sense of relief, here was no Ben to disturb her hardwon peace of mind; less exuberant than Dale, there was nevertheless something very attractive and reassuring about him. Within seconds they were chatting away almost like old friends, and it wasn't until she saw Dale frowning that Sarah felt a tiny shiver of apprehension dance along her skin. 'Dale, is something wrong?' she asked hesitantly. It wasn't exactly unheard-of for petty quarrels and jealousies to develop in the tightly knit community involved in the making of any film, but the Dale she remembered had always been able to smile and shrug off these small unpleasantnesses. And yet, old friends though they were, it was practically unheard-of for a principal member of the cast to come and pick up a rather minor one. It was almost as though Dale had taken the opportunity to do so quite deliberately. Paul, too, looked rather grave, and as Sarah glanced from one face to the other, Paul suggested tactfully, 'I'll put the luggage in the car.'

'I came to pick you up because I wanted to have a word with you, Sarah,' Dale told her. 'Well, more to warn you really . . .'

'Warn me?' Sarah could feel tension coiling along her spine.

'Umm, Paul insisted on coming with me, which was rather a nuisance. Judging by the looks he was giving you I shouldn't be at all surprised if he wants to extend your relationship beyond the confines of a working one. What do you think of him?'

Sarah tried not to feel too exasperated. 'We've only just met,' she protested. 'He seems very pleasant, but I'm not in the market for personal relationships—you know that, Dale.'

'Umm, just checking.' But the smile he gave her was understanding and friendly. 'Look, Paul will be back in a second, and I'd better tell you before he comes. We've got a new director . . .' He paused and Sarah felt her heartstrings jerk and tighten indefinably with tension.

'I thought Guy was going to direct, himself?' she protested shakily.

'So he was,' Dale agreed bitterly, 'and if I'd known any different, I wouldn't have taken the damned part, but it seems something went wrong on his last film, and he's having to re-shoot several scenes. The backers demanded it, and because everything was set up here, and any delay now would mean waiting until next summer, we've got ourselves a new director.' He glanced at her as Paul closed the car boot and started walking towards them.

'It's Ben, Sarah,' he told her quickly, his hand going to her arm as he saw her sway slightly. 'Look, I know what a shock this must be to you, that's why I wanted to be the first to tell you. Knowing that bastard, he'd just let you walk right into him without any preparation at all. You must

have done quite well out of him when the divorce
went through.' He gave her an oblique look. 'I
mean, by that time he'd have been working in
America; he went there right after *Shakespeare*
finished, didn't he?'

Sarah made no response—she wasn't capable of
doing so. Ben directing *Richard*—she couldn't
believe it! She didn't want to believe it. Paul came
to join them, and if he found anything strange in
her pale face and strained features, he was too
polite to say so, simply opening the front
passenger door of the car for her when she reached
it, and helping her with her seat-belt, causing Dale
to raise an eyebrow and comment that he
obviously believed in working himself into the
right mood for a part. 'Not that you'll find Sarah
a walk-over,' he added, grinning at Sarah
encouragingly. 'She knows all about the dangers of
getting involved with her leading men, don't you,
sweetling?'

Sarah knew that Dale was only teasing her, but
she wished he had been a little more reticent when
she saw the way Paul looked at her. 'Some of them
have caused problems,' she agreed lightly.

'And in case you think she means me, Sarah and
I have always had a very special relationship,
haven't we?' Dale chipped in.

They had in many ways, and Sarah grinned
back at him, trying to banish from her mind the
knowledge that soon she was going to come face
to face with Ben, Ben whose acting ability in
Shakespeare had been so greatly acclaimed, but
who had gone on to find equal fame in directing
and producing. She could vouch personally for his

acting ability; she had had first-hand personal
experience of it. She smiled rather bitterly to
herself. God, how naïve she had been! Dale had
been a good friend to her then. If it hadn't been
for him she would never have known the truth;
never known how cruelly Ben had deceived her.
She had thought he loved her as she loved him
while all she had really been to him was the
fulfilment of a bet. Even now to think about what
had happened brought her flesh out in goose-
bumps, shivering with distaste and despair. Dale,
frantic when he learned that Ben had married her,
had told her the truth, wanting to protect her; Ben
with whom she was so crazily and deeply in love
had married her for no other reason than simply
to win a bet. It had started in complete innocence,
on Dale's part at least. When the three of them
started to film *Shakespeare*, Dale had bet Ben a
thousand pounds that he would be the first one to
get her into bed, and Ben had accepted the wager.
When he had told her of his own part in what had
happened Dale had had the grace to be very
shamefaced, but he had not known her then; she
had just been another very pretty girl and the bet
had been made half in jest, but already there had
been a certain competitiveness between himself
and Ben; Dale being the more acclaimed and well-
known actor of the two, and Ben had obviously
determined that this time he was going to be the
winner.

Sarah had had no idea about the bet between
her two fellow actors; no idea of what was
intended, and while from the very first she had
been wary of Dale's outrageously flirtatious

manner and had kept him at bay, she had had no defences against her own feelings for Benedict, falling in love with him almost at first sight, allowing herself to become so bemused by him and their roles that she had permitted him to make love to her, and she had thought when she had refused to allow him to make their relationship public that his proposal of marriage stemmed from his desire and love for her, not realising that he simply saw it as the only way he could force Dale to acknowledge that he was the winner of their bet.

Dale had been enjoying a brief break away from the set when it happened and only returned the day they were married by special licence, less than a week after Ben had made love to her. Dale had got slightly drunk at the post-wedding party given by the cast, and he had followed up to her hotel room when she went to get changed, to tell her the truth. Sarah had still been in tears when they heard Ben outside the door, and it had been then that Dale had whispered to her that they would turn the tables on him, taking her in his arms and wrenching unfastened the front of her dress so that Ben had discovered them together locked in what appeared to be an intensely passionate embrace, Dale's cool comment that he had after all lost, as Sarah preferred him, driving Benedict from the room and ultimately from her life. She could still vividly remember the climax to their wedding party when Ben very obviously drunk, had announced to the assembled cast that she and Dale were lovers.

She thought guiltily about Dale's comment on their divorce. She always described herself as 'divorced', but the plain facts of the matter were

that she was still, legally at least, married to Ben.
They had been married in England, where the law
had been and still was that only an uncontested
divorce could be obtained after three years. Where
both parties were not in agreement the waiting
period was five years, and it was still only three
and a half years since they had been married. Why
Ben refused to give her a divorce she had no idea,
unless it was because he feared she might make
some sort of financial claim on him. Either that, or
he simply wanted to punish her. But she wasn't the
guilty party. She had married him because she was
deeply in love with him and had believed he felt
the same way about her. Their love scenes together
had possessed an intensity, a luminosity which had
far transcended even the most gifted acting, or so
she had believed, and driven half mad by her love
for him and the constant exposure to the
sensuality imposed on them by their roles, she had
abandoned all her dearly held beliefs—and
herself—to him.

The screech of the car brakes jerked her back to
the present. Dale had always been an aggressive
driver and in that regard he didn't seem to have
changed.

'I've just been telling Sarah about our new
director,' he commented to Paul. 'Unlike me,' he
added for Sarah's benefit, 'Paul likes our new
director. Of course he isn't the only one. Gina, my
sweetly innocent Berengaria, had made her
preferences in that quarter very well known. Of
course Ben's playing it cool—he can hardly do
otherwise since Gina's lover is one of our most
influential backers. He's having quite a hard time of

it trying to keep Gina at bay without offending her, but then he always was adept at double-dealing. Still, you're going to come as quite a shock to him.'

From the back seat Paul interrupted gently, 'A very pleasant one, I'm sure, Sarah. It's just that there's been a change on the continuity side as well, and the girl who replaced Ellen, our first continuity girl, must have forgotten to take Rachel Ware's name out and insert yours in the casting list.'

Sarah's heart sank even further. She hadn't realised that someone else had actually been cast for the part ahead of her. 'Come on, Dale,' Paul protested. 'You're frightening the life out of Sarah! Ben won't eat you,' he told her. 'Oh, he's demanding all right—knows exactly what he wants from the cast and makes sure he gets it, but . . .'

'Sarah knows all about Ben, Paul,' Dale interrupted, his eyes leaving the road for a second as he turned his head to frown at the man in the back seat. 'We both worked with him on *Shakespeare*. You'll have to forgive Paul's ignorance,' he added to Sarah. 'He's come rather late to the acting scene. He was training to be a chartered accountant when he suddenly got the bug.'

'I qualified, too,' Paul put in with a disarming grin. 'I had a girl-friend who was a model, and she got me some ad work, which is how I got started.'

'Yes, he's the original chocolate-box hero,' Dale retorted.

So Paul didn't know about her marriage to Ben; of course it was over three years ago and had happened in England, and Sarah couldn't help hoping that the rest of the cast were similarly ignorant. It wasn't going to be easy working with him, especially not with the eyes of the rest of the cast monitoring their responses to one another.

'Is it much further?' Sarah queried, trying to ease the crick in her neck. They seemed to have been speeding through the dark, apparently empty countryside, for half a lifetime, and on top of her flight, the journey was beginning to take its toll on her.

'Only another ten miles or so,' Paul comforted her from the back.

'If Guy wasn't such a fanatic for realism we could have shot most of these scenes in the Californian desert and used the studios for everything else,' Dale chimed in rather bitterly.

Telling herself that it was only natural that Dale should sound a little disgruntled, after all Hollywood was home to him now and he must have grown accustomed to all the luxuries it offered, Sarah wondered what he would say if she confided to him how thrilled she was that they *were* filming on location.

'Well, here we are,' Dale announced fifteen minutes later as he pulled off the main road and they bumped down a dusty, narrow track.

Ahead of them a collection of lights shone from the windows of large trailers, and the guard on duty at the makeshift 'gate' grinned a welcome to Dale, eyeing Sarah with a flat curiosity that made her raise her eyebrows a little. 'He obviously thinks I'm someone you've picked up for the evening,' she commented to Dale as he parked his car outside a darkened trailer and Paul got out, having wished them both goodnight,

'*And* he's probably envying me,' Dale retorted with a grin, coming round to open her door. 'By the way,' he added casually, 'one of the problems we have here is that we're a little short on accommodation at the moment. Will you slap my face, sweetling, if I suggest you share with me for tonight? There's a separate bedroom, and rather than rouse half the outfit . . .'

Hiding her surprise, Sarah nodded her agreement. A glance at her watch showed her that it was after one in the morning, and her body ached for sleep. She knew Dale well enough to know that she could trust him, and although she had half expected to have to share a trailer—accommodation always being notoriously problematical on location—she had reckoned on sharing with one of the other girls.

'You were to have shared with Gina,' Dale explained to her as he extracted a key from his pocket and unlocked the metal door, flicking on the light as he did so, and allowing Sarah to step past him into the illuminated interior, 'but our dear Garia kicked up a fuss. It seems that sharing with someone would not be convenient—unless of course that someone happens to be our director. However, Ben isn't playing—at least not publicly. With all the other problems he's got on his hands, I don't suppose he's any too keen to upset one of our backers. He's going to have a hard time of it, trying to appease both Gina and her lover. He could, of course, always bow out and let someone else take over, but his last film wasn't exactly a box-office winner and . . .'

'Oh, but surely,' Sarah broke in impulsively,

without thinking, 'it got the Best Film Award, and . . .'

'It might have got the Award, sweetling,' Dale told her dryly, 'but if you want my opinion, Ben over-stepped himself, spending so much on making it, and that money won't be easily recouped. Would you like a drink before I show you to your room, madam?' he parodied, laughing at her, as he changed the subject and indicated one of the three doors leading off the narrow corridor which ran from the living area in which they were standing, and down past a small but very highly sophisticated kitchen.

'If you don't mind, I think I'll go straight to bed,' Sarah told him, suddenly conscious of the hectic day behind her, fulfilling the last of her ad commitments, and the long journey to their destination. 'Are you sure you don't mind putting me up for tonight, Dale, I could . . .'

Was there a touch of impatience in the frown lining his forehead? Dale was probably tired, too, and she was fussing unnecessarily, Sarah told herself when he assured her that he didn't.

'Come on, you can have this room. I'll say this for Guy,' he added as he pushed open the door, 'these trailers are well equipped, even down to air-conditioning. He even had a temporary pool installed on the site. Not that we get much chance to use it with dear old Ben in charge. He's a real slavedriver!' He slanted Sarah a sideways glance, and her scalp prickled with sensitive awareness. There had always been keen competition between the two men, but now she sensed that this had changed, deepened in some way, and this suspicion was confirmed when Dale said slowly, 'He's changed since we filmed *Shakespeare* together, Sarah, and much as I hate to say it, he's a sore loser. Don't worry about it, though,' he told her, his expression lightening, 'Uncle Dale's here to protect you.'

Was the air-conditioning the sole reason she was shivering? Sarah wondered half an hour later as she prepared for bed in the small but luxurious 'room' Dale had given her. It was senseless unpacking until she discovered where she was to stay, so, having showered in Dale's minute but compact bathroom, she pulled on the nightdress she had extracted from one of her cases and climbed into bed.

It was silly to feel so apprehensive simply because she was working with Ben again. He would want to forget the past as much as she did. Hadn't he said when he stormed out of their room on the night of the party that he never wanted to set eyes on her again? So why hadn't he agreed to their divorce? Perhaps Dale was right and he was worried that she might make a huge financial claim on him—after all, he was now a very successful and presumably wealthy man. Her face tightened in disgust. He had indeed changed if he thought she would take a single penny from him. All she wanted was her freedom.

She sighed, remembering how she had fretted over the difficulty in getting a divorce. Her solicitor had been patient, but clearly a little at a loss.

'Is there someone else you want to marry?' he had enquired, and when Sarah shook her head had looked both thoughtful and perplexed, pointing out that the waiting period was meant to give couples a chance to see if they could not bury their differences and make a go of their marriages. A tight fist seemed to grip her heart, squeezing it until the pain was almost more than she could endure. What was the matter? Sarah asked herself bitterly. Surely she had learned long ago the folly of loving Ben? Hadn't his treatment of her then— seducing her and then marrying her simply to get one up on Dale—killed all she had ever felt for him? So why did she feel this nerve-clenching sense of apprehension, and yes, anticipation at the thought of seeing him?

Too tired to find an answer to the riddle, she fell into an exhausted sleep.

The unfamiliar noises of the site woke her, and Sarah opened her eyes slowly, sitting upright when she remembered where she was. She glanced at her watch. Just gone seven, and already, if the sounds she could hear were any indication, the day's work was well under way.

Showering quickly, she returned to her room to pull on a checked cotton shirt and some ancient jeans, brushing her hair quickly and securing it off her face with a band. The first thing she had to do was to find Ben's assistant, report in to him or her and find out when she would be needed for filming.

Fortunately the weeks in between learning that she had got the part and her arrival in Spain had given her enough time to learn her lines, although she was fully prepared to find that some of them might have been changed in the interim. Would

the mysterious author of the film script be in
evidence? It wasn't entirely unheard-of for writers
to want to be present when their work was filmed,
and since apparently the writer had also done the
film script it was perfectly feasible that he would
be on site. Sarah's stomach tightened in a small
thrill of anticipation and, chiding herself for being
too impressionable, she quickly packed up her
things and straightened the bed. It was almost as
though she had a crush on the man—and without
knowing the first thing about him! But that wasn't
true, she admitted thoughtfully. She *did* know
about him. It was impossible to read the script and
not be aware that he was a man of considerable
compassion; of deeply felt but perhaps sometimes
hidden emotions; a man to whom loyalty and self-
respect meant far more than the indulgence in
momentary pleasure.

There was no sign of Dale when she emerged
from her room, and not knowing whether he was
still asleep or already working, Sarah found the
coffee percolator and filled it almost automatically,
unable to resist the temptation to open the door
and enjoy the lazy warmth of the morning as she
waited for it to be ready. Later on the heat might
be oppressive, especially if she was working, but
right now it was just perfect, the tender fingers of
morning sunshine warming the bare skin of her
throat and arms, making her want to bask like a
lazy cat. She closed her eyes languorously, opening
them again quickly as a shadow blotted out the
warmth of the sun, some sixth sense alerting her,
awareness prickling dangerously over her skin as
her muscles tightened and she saw that the object

that had come between herself and the sun was
none other than her husband, Benedict de l'Isle,
director and producer and the Most Important
Man under God on the site.

He saw her at the same moment as she saw him,
halting almost mid-stride, a look, almost of shock,
rippling across features that looked as though they
had been hewn from stone. If Dale was the
archetype of fair-headed good looks, his face open
and sunny, then Ben was his direct opposite,
Lucifer fallen to earth with his darkly bitter
features, his hair as black as night, and his profile
that of a man to whom the weaknesses of others
were unknown. Eyes the colour of jade assessed
her ruthlessly, stripping away the veneer of
sophistication she had gathered over the years, and
with it the barrier of her clothes, so that Sarah felt
as though she stood before him as she had done on
the set for *Shakespeare*, naked, and vulnerable.
And then she remembered that Dale had told her
Ben didn't know she was among the cast. That
gave her enough courage to lift her head and
match him stare for stare. Her heart hammered
violently against the confines of her flesh. She had
forgotten how tall he was. She was five eight and
even with the advantage of the steps she still had
to look up to him. The surprise, if indeed there
had been any, was gone, and had been replaced by
the same icy contempt she remembered from
another confrontation. It was really amazing how
green eyes could be so cold, she thought, shivering
a little as she realised the interested stares they
were attracting from the small crowd that seemed
to have gathered almost instinctively, drawn by the

scent of blood no doubt, she thought bitterly.
Well, if Ben thought he was going to take this part
away from her! Her eyes smouldered darkly. She
needed it far too much to give it up tamely, and
she had her contract . . .

With a little start she realised that already she
was on the defensive, feeling too vulnerable, too
aware of the power of the man watching her.

She shivered again as Ben's mouth curled
tauntingly, stepping backwards and instantly
grateful for the warm support of Dale's arm, as it
curved round her. She hadn't realised he was
there, Paul at his side, and the brief glance she
gave him showed that she was tremulously glad of
his presence.

'Morning, Ben,' he drawled affably. 'Come to
say hello to your ex-wife?'

Sarah saw Paul's eyes widen, but barely had
time to register her protest of Dale's unwise
comment, her swiftly indrawn breath checked as
Ben's face darkened, his eyes and mouth hard with
contempt. What on earth had possessed Dale to
challenge him like that? Paul too looked to be
concerned and slightly shocked. Obviously he had
meant well, but Sarah shivered, wishing he had
kept quiet.

'My ex-wife?' Ben murmured softly, cruelty
glinting in the smile he gave Sarah as he reached
them, grasping her hand, and uncurling fingers
almost numb with shock as he jerked her forward
so that she practically fell into his arms.

'You mean to say you haven't told him,
darling?'

The words were murmured against her ear,

shivering across her skin, Ben's hold tightening
round her until she could barely breathe. Almost
as though she were standing outside herself Sarah
witnessed the small tableau—Dale, standing in the
doorway of the trailer, wary, and questioning, his
eyes searching her face as he tested it for reaction.
Ben and herself locked in an embrace which made
her frighteningly aware of the muscled power of
his body, her back and legs warmed by the male
flesh of his body, the contrast of his darkly tanned
forearm resting alongside the pale fragility of hers,
his fingers curling possessively round her wrist,
holding it just before the curve of her breasts, so
that he couldn't help but be aware of the hurried
thud of her heart.

'Told me what?' Dale demanded at length with
just enough edge under the light voice he used for
Sarah to know that he was taken off guard.

'Why, simply that she isn't and never has been
my "ex",' Ben drawled lightly, the concerted but
very audible gasp that went up from their
'audience' reminding Sarah that he always had
been a first-rate actor, able to draw every last
ounce of emotion out of any scene.

'You could have told Dale our little secret,
darling,' Ben murmured behind her. She felt him
bend his head, and then the warm brush of his
mouth against her skin, just below her ear, making
her shiver in shocked response. 'I know I said I
didn't want it made public just yet, but since I
took this job especially to be near you, I think
we've rather given ourselves away, don't you?'

Sarah was too numb to speak. She couldn't
bring herself to look at Dale. How could she deny

Ben's assertion that she was still his wife, when in effect it was perfectly true? But as for the rest of his statement! She tugged away from him, her eyes already darkening with anger, and thought she had caught him off guard as she found herself free, but her freedom only extended to the length of time it took Ben to turn her in his arms, so that her breasts were crushed against the thin silk of his shirt, her nostrils full of the male scent of him, the grainy texture of his skin, and the hard pressure of his body as he held her against him.

'For those of you who don't know,' he drawled, raising his voice so that it reached the crowd of onlookers, now much larger than it had originally been and every one of them unashamedly listening, 'Sarah and I have been separated for the past few years, but now we're back together again, and my only regret is that on this occasion I won't be playing her lover—at least not in public!'

There was a wave of goodnatured laughter, only Dale and Sarah not joining in. She couldn't believe this, Sarah thought dazedly. Why had he done it? And then as she heard him saying coolly, 'I didn't realise you were arriving last night, darling. You should have let me know. Never mind, you're here now. I'll get someone to move your things to my trailer. Thanks for looking after her, Dale. It's almost like old times,' she knew. He wasn't going to have it said a second time that his wife had a lover who wasn't her husband. But why not simply divorce her? He didn't want her. He had made that more than plain enough; had told her to go to Dale. She could still remember the cruelty of his words when he had done so. All she had ever been to him had been the winning of a bet!

The crowd was slowly beginning to drift away. Break-ups and reconciliations were common enough in their industry not to cause too much comment, although it would have seriously undermined Ben's authority had it been thought that his estranged wife was having an affair with another member of the cast.

'Let me go!' Sarah demanded tersely, not even bothering to conceal the shaken anger she was feeling. Dale was still watching them and came down the steps, frowning as he approached them.

'Look, Sarah, if . . .'

'Leave it, Dale,' Ben cut in in clipped accents. 'Like I said, I'll have someone move Sarah's things to my trailer. You're supposed to be filming in half an hour, aren't you?' he added, flicking a glance at his watch. 'They'll be waiting for you in Make-up.'

Faced with what was tantamount to an order, Dale had little alternative but to go, and Sarah watched him leave, anger and anguish mingled in her eyes as Ben retained his hold on her until Dale was swallowed up in the dust and heat of the morning.

'Well now,' he drawled when Dale had gone, 'are you going to tell me what you were doing spending the night in his trailer, or can I guess?'

'You *can*,' Sarah spat back, 'but if you judge Dale and me by your own standards, then you wouldn't come within a mile of the truth! And speaking of motives, Ben, why did you announce that we were reconciled?'

'We've got to work together, Sarah. I want to

make a success of this film, and I'm not having the cast and crew more interested in gossiping about us than in doing a first-rate job.'

'But no one need even have known that we were married,' Sarah bit out. 'I . . .'

'I quite agree,' Ben cut in tersely, 'and who have we to thank for the fact that they do know?'

For a moment Sarah looked at him blankly, then she remembered Dale announcing her as Ben's 'ex-wife'. 'Dale didn't mean anything,' she said uncomfortably. 'You know what he's like.'

'Probably better than you,' came the crisply derisive response, 'but the damage is done now, Sarah. I've got enough problems on my hands already without you and Dale stirring up more. I'd feel much happier if you weren't here to add to them, but failing that, it will make life that little bit easier for me to have you under my eye, where I can see you. And, Sarah . . .' She turned to look at him, dry-mouthed with apprehension at the tone of his voice. 'Any attempt on your part to resume your affair with Dale, and I'll get myself another Joanna, contract or no contract, understand?'

Just for a second she toyed with the idea of telling him what he could do with his part, but she needed it too much; needed and wanted it. Ever since she had read the script she had known how much she wanted to be in the film. Not just because it was destined to be an out-and-out success, but because something about the way it was written, the development of the characters, struck a sympathetic chord deep inside her.

'I don't want to share a trailer with you,' she heard herself saying childishly, knowing that they both knew that she had given in. 'I . . .'

'I'm not exactly thrilled about it myself,' Ben
agreed curtly, 'but needs must, and anyway, we've
nowhere else to put you.'

'Because Gina insists on having a trailer to
herself. Why don't you simply share with her, and
let me have your trailer?' Sarah suggested sweetly.
'That way you'll be keeping both your main
actresses happy.'

'Dale *has* been busy, hasn't he?' was Ben's only
comment, but Sarah hadn't missed the way his
eyes narrowed, nor the dark flush running along
the high cheekbones. Somehow her comment had
got to him, which in itself was worthy of further
investigation. Was he not as immune to Gina as he
pretended? 'Well, just try to remember that this
time you're playing brother and sister, and not
lovers. And if you want to blame someone because
you're having to share with me, then blame Dale—
after all, he's the one who announced that we were
married.' He glanced at his watch again. 'I'm due
on set in ten minutes. You'll find my trailer on the
far side of the camp. It's on its own—a brown and
cream monstrosity, you can't miss it. By the way,'
he added, halting her and pinning her where she
stood with the icy intentness of his scrutiny, 'how
come you changed the time of your flight? I had
fully intended to come and collect you myself.'

'You had? But . . .'

Two facts hit her simultaneously. One was that
Dale had been wrong and that Ben had known she
was to play Joanna. The other was that someone
had obviously misled him over her flight, because
she had certainly not altered it.

'But?' he encouraged, still watching her. 'But you and Dale decided it would create more of an impact if you were seen with him? Nice try, Sarah, but this time you've been out-manoeuvred.'

'Because you lied about us being reconciled,' Sarah said bitterly, ignoring the accusation he had tossed at her. 'Reconciled!' She laughed acidly. 'You never even wanted to marry me in the first place—you . . .'

'But I did,' Ben cut in grimly, 'and having done so, I'm having to pay for my mistake—just like you—and be warned, Sarah, this time I'm not going to allow you and Dale to make a laughing-stock out of me!'

He was gone before she could retort, striding through the heat and dust-hazed morning, the rigid line of his disappearing back reminding Sarah of the hard pressure of his body against hers. In Dale she had seen few changes if any to mark the intervening years; in Ben she saw many. As Southampton he had won acclaim for his acting ability, and had been more of a heart-throb than Dale, his darkly macho good looks causing more of an impact on the audience. He had been just thirty when they met. Now he was thirty-three, going on thirty-four, and like something cast in iron, he had hardened rather than mellowed. Oh, he was still good-looking—Sarah closed her eyes, quivering in recognition of the sexual appeal that nothing could destroy, and she hadn't been immune to it. Held prisoner in his arms, it had been fatally easy to remember how it had been between them, and even if there had not been the love she believed at the time, there had still been the passion and desire. If she closed her eyes she could still feel the echoes of it now, tongues of flame licking through her veins, the weak wanting in the pit of her stomach; the need to touch and taste the male flesh against her own. She opened her eyes, half dizzy from the emotions she fought to control, telling herself that it was the sunshine that made her feel so weak and disorientated. She glanced around her and sighed, wishing with all her heart that Guy Holland was still directing the film. Just for a moment she contemplated breaking her contract, and then her fighting instinct came to the fore. Ben probably expected her to run from him like a frightened rabbit—just as Mary Fitton had run from Southampton—well, she would show him! Before she could change her mind she swung round on her heel and headed in the direction Ben had pointed out to her.

Before she got to Ben's trailer, Sarah found the trailers which were being used as the administrative offices for the unit. One of the four girls working there, a plump, cheerful brunette, produced a work schedule, adding by way of warning, 'Of course it changes from day to day—you know what it's like—but we'll be pinning a fresh one up here every morning, and of course if you're in any doubt, you're lucky, you can always check with the boss at night!' Her ready smile robbed the words of any offence, and when Sarah smiled back the girl gave a relieved grin and extended a small capable hand. 'I haven't introduced myself, by the way. I'm Lois and the others are Anne, Helen and Sue, respectively. Thank goodness you're human. After all the tantrums we've had from Madame

Gina we were getting a bit worried about you, especially after this morning's surprise. We had no idea the boss was married, much less to one of our leading ladies.'

'We've been separated for some time,' Sarah told her, unwilling to discuss her relationship with Ben and yet unwilling to offend by seeming aloof.

'We all envy you like mad,' Lois confided with another grin, 'and my, oh my, won't our Gina be surprised! She got him earmarked as her private property, and he must be relieved that she'll have to back down a little now that you've arrived. Anything going on between the two of them was bound to cause unpleasant repercussions if it ever got back to the ears of her boy-friend. He's one of our backers,' she added by way of clarification, and Sarah didn't tell her that Dale had already informed her of this relationship. 'Guy fought damned hard to get the money for this film, and we're all relieved that Ben agreed to take over from him. It's hard enough getting money out of backers these days to produce a film, without having to contend with a director who's a yes-man and cuts corners and costs at every turn.'

Sarah could see that the other girl thought highly of Ben, which she knew from past experience was an accolade in itself. The crew were notorious for being 'anti' directors, and if a director did command their respect one could be sure that it had been hard won.

Half an hour later, having accepted the cup of coffee Lois offered, Sarah opened the door of Ben's trailer. Slightly larger than Dale's, it was on its own away from the others. Privileges of power,

Sarah thought wryly, wondering why Ben had opted for seclusion. So that Gina could visit him unnoticed? She told herself she was being stupid, especially in view of all that she had been told, and anyway, why should it concern her if Gina and Ben had an affair?

Unlike Dale's, the living area of the trailer was cluttered with mounds of paper. A typewriter sat uncovered on the table, and Sarah glanced curiously at it. The administration unit was fully equipped with all manner of electronic marvels, including a word processor, and she couldn't understand why Ben should need a machine in his own living accommodation. Shrugging her shoulders, she investigated the doors leading off the corridor. One opened on to a kitchen very like Dale's, only larger, with a breakfast bar in it. Next to it was a bathroom, and guessing that Ben would choose the bedroom nearest to it, Sarah pushed open the other door, into what was patently the unused bedroom.

Most of her luggage was still in Dale's car, and since she couldn't unpack she might as well make herself some belated breakfast and then explore the set. A swift glance at the schedule Lois had given her confirmed that she would not be needed until towards the end of the week, but she noticed that she had a wardrobe consultation first thing in the morning, and doubtless there would be many other things to fill in her time.

Half an hour later, having breakfasted on toast and coffee, and cleaned up after herself, she decided it was time to make her tour of the site, and familiarise herself with what was going to be her home for the next two or three months.

CHAPTER THREE

THE film company must have several million dollars tied up in the location site alone, Sarah decided, pausing to marvel at the swimming pool which had been dug in the sand and formed from some sort of plasticised liner. At one end a bar had been erected, complete with a 'coconut matting' roof and realistically weathered tables and chairs. To one side of it was a partially open restaurant where she guessed most of the crew and cast would take their meals, although it was possible to be entirely self-sufficient by using the freezer and fridge built into the trailer kitchens. A dozen or so people were seated outside the bar, the men drinking beer and the girls a mixture of the former and lemonade, reminding Sarah that the Spanish climate was a hot one and that she would be wise to protect her complexion from it. She did not need to be told how important it was not to let her skin burn—apart from the undoubted pain of doing so it could have a disastrous effect on any film shot out of sequence—she could hardly appear pale-skinned at the beginning of a scene, and then bright pink halfway through it.

She ought to have bought herself a sunhat before leaving England, but there had been so much to do she had forgotten it. She did have plenty of sunscreen, thanks to Carew, but she would need a hat if she was not to suffer from sunstroke. It wasn't even midday yet and the heat was almost suffocating. She glanced longingly at the pool, and then reminded herself that she was here to work, not play. She would go and watch the shooting, she decided on impulse. She had never seen Ben direct and it would be as well to discover what type of method he adopted—whether it was of the 'stick' or 'carrot' variety. It was a well known maxim in Hollywood circles that the better the director the more his cast loathed him. Suppressing a shiver, Sarah wound her way through the seemingly haphazard arrangement of trailers back to the administration centre.

'You want to know where they're filming? Sure,' Lois agreed laconically. 'Why not come with me? I've got to take some stuff out for the boss. We'll take one of the buggies.' She glanced at Sarah's uncovered head. 'Go ahead and tell me if I'm stepping out of line, but shouldn't you be wearing a hat, your being a redhead an' all?'

'I would if I'd had the sense to buy one in London,' Sarah agreed ruefully. 'First thing tomorrow I must find someone to take me to the nearest town so that I can buy one. Will anyone be going in?'

Lois shook her head regretfully. 'I doubt it. There's nothing in the can for sending off. We've been having problems with one of the cameras, but it's okay now and the boss said only yesterday that he didn't want anyone sneaking off to town—we've got too much lost time to catch up on. I expect he'll make allowances for you, though,' she told Sarah with a sideways grin. 'He won't want one of his leading ladies to go down with

sunstroke—nor his wife to suffer from a headache!'
She laughed when she saw Sarah's expression.
'Honey, you're going to have to toughen up some
if you're going to survive on location. You haven't
done much film work, I guess?' she hazarded
sympathetically. 'Some of the guys don't mince
their words. You should have heard them this
morning when they found out about you! Word is
that you must be some lady to have been able to
tie the boss down. I guess it's not exactly news to
you that the fact that he's one very virile man
hasn't gone unnoticed in Tinsel Town.'

Sarah smiled and said nothing. Of course she
hadn't expected Ben to live the life of a monk
when they separated, so why this curious pang of
something that could almost be called pain, slicing
through her body, cutting through her defences
and leaving her aching and vulnerable to the
white-hot pangs of jealousy ripping through her?

Lois led the way to a beach buggy parked not
far away. 'The film crew have commandeered most
of the jeeps,' she explained briefly, 'but these little
guys are far better than any car in the rough.'

'What are they filming today?' Sarah asked,
trying to remember what she had seen on the
schedule. Hadn't it been some part of the Crusade;
just before Richard ordered the execution of his
Muslim hostages?

When she questioned Lois, the other girl agreed.
'Originally the boss hoped to have it in the can by
last week, but with the camera out of action ...
There's an old castle out here that we're using as
part of the set. At the moment it's standing in for
the walls of Acre.'

Sarah knew from the script that in reprisal for refusing to release his Christian prisoners and to pay the ransom demanded of him, Richard had punished the Muslim leader Salah-ed-Din by putting to the sword the Muslim prisoners the Christian forces had taken when they captured Acre. For a Christian knight it was a barbaric act, especially when he had made his wife and sister witness it, but then Richard had been reputed to have a temper to match his red-gold hair, and Salah-ed-Din's refusal to accede to his demands must have infuriated him, but Sarah knew that the script, while faithfully following actual events, had allowed a little fiction to creep in along with the death of one of the fictional characters, Richard's lover, the knight Philip, who had left Richard on Cyprus to join the Knights Templar, a celibate fighting order, in order to do penance for their sin. This knight had been captured by a band of ferocious warriors known as 'Assassins', a title derived from the fact that they ate the hashish drug. From her own careful research, Sarah knew that it was quite true that the stronghold of the Knights Templar had been attacked by the Assassins and that many had been killed in the hills surrounding the citadel.

She also knew that this scene now to be shot was the culmination of Richard's relationship with his lover. Salah-ed-Din, unwilling to pay the ransom Richard demanded for the return of his prisoners, had instead offered to Richard the life of his lover. Richard had refused, and at the appointed time when Salah-ed-Din should have sent his ransom to the Christian camp, instead he

had sent a dying man, his body tied to one of the
creamy pale Arabian horses so greatly valued by
the Moors, blood pouring from the wound in his
side.

Declining to accompany Lois when she went
across to Ben, Sarah attached herself to a group of
extras just off set. The ancient castle was decrepit
enough to have an air of authenticity, its walls half
crumbling into the dusty sand, the sun glittering
hotly on the pale stone.

A line of brightly striped pavilions had been
erected at the base of the walls; the tents of the
Christian army. Some distance away were another
group of tents, this time representing those of the
Muslim forces, and it was in a mock-up of one of
these that the filming was taking place.

The actor playing the Muslim leader sat
impassive and cross-legged before a small brazier,
white-robed and impressive, half a dozen feroci-
ously warlike attendants at his back.

Seated opposite him on a small stool, arms
folded across his chest, sat Dale, and Sarah caught
her breath at the change in him. Make-up and
period clothes had transformed him into exactly
what she had visualised Richard to be. Contact
lenses had changed his grey eyes to steely blue, and
watching him, Sarah found it hard to believe that
he *wasn't* Richard in the flesh, her vivid
imagination instantly transporting her back in
time to the twelfth century, her senses instantly
responsive to the scene being played out before
her.

Salah-ed-Din was speaking, his voice even and
devoid of all expression, his smile cruelly mocking,

as he murmured softly, 'It is indeed regrettable,
Lord Richard, that we have not as yet been able to
collect the full sum of the ransom you demand.'
He shrugged fatalistically. 'We are a poor people,
and have to squeeze the money out like water from
the desert.'

'With a ruby on your finger the size of a
pigeon's egg?' Richard mocked. 'You know my
terms. If the hostages and the money are not paid
over within the month, the garrison of Acre shall
be put to the sword.'

The Muslim leader laughed softly. 'Ah, Richard.
Always so sure; so frank! But I think this time I shall
be the victor. Why should I pay you good money
when there are other ways? The Chief of the
Assassins has lately sent me a gift. I would show it to
you,' He clapped his hands and Sarah found she was
holding her breath, her throat and chest hurting
even though she knew what was coming.

'Is it true that the French King leaves us?' the
Muslim enquired as his bodyguard disappeared.

'You are behind the times,' Richard responded.
'He has already gone.'

There was some commotion beyond the tent,
and Sarah gritted her teeth, one half of her
knowing that she was being stupid because none of
what she was seeing was real, the other half totally
caught up in what was happening.

'Ah, here is my gift,' the Muslim leader
exclaimed in gentle satisfaction as his men
reappeared, carrying what on first sight appeared
to be a bundle of rags. 'Bring it here so that the
Lord King may view it better,' Salah-ed-Din
commanded softly.

Instantly obedient, his bodyguards tumbled the bundle on to the floor. A man lay there, his pale skin heavily bruised, blood staining the palms of his hands, his breathing shallow, the dark hair disordered and the white tunic bearing the Cross of the Knights of Malta dusty and torn.

'Lift his head.'

Sarah glanced at Richard. He was totally absorbed in the man before him, dark colour running up under his ruddy skin, fingers biting into the palms of his hands.

'The Assassins were curious to witness the method by which the prophet you call Jesus died,' Salah-ed-Din told Richard softly. 'Fortunately I managed to curb their enthusiasm before it went too far.'

The camera panned on to the bloodstained palms, the torn surplice with the slit along the side, thickly encrusted with blood, and Sarah shivered despite the heat of the afternoon.

'He will not know you, Lord Richard.' The words came softly, tenderly almost. 'He has been given the drug hashish. Our physicians can save him. You have only to give the word. This man whom you so dearly love—you hold his life in your palm. I will give him to you instead of the ransom.'

'No!'

The word was ripped from Richard's throat, his face a tortured mask. Sarah discovered she was holding her breath again, this time her palms wet with sweat.

'No?' Salah-ed-Din questioned.

'No,' Richard repeated more firmly, with less

anguish. 'Were the terms of our treaty only one dinar and one prisoner, they could not be altered, nor would he wish me to do so.' He bent forward and touched the dark hair yearningly, wiping the blood from the cut lips before pressing his own against them in brief agony, and then turned to leave the tent, throwing curtly over his shoulder, 'You have fourteen days to find the ransom money.'

'Phew!' Behind her Sarah heard someone let out a pent-up breath. 'Gut-gripping stuff,' someone else agreed, and there was general laughter in the release from tension.

'Can it, Rick,' Sarah heard Ben saying coolly as he strolled up to Dale.

'Satisfied, oh master?' Sarah heard Dale demand caustically, adding, 'God, Ben, I'm not doing it again. I've already sweated blood over this scene!'

'And came up with a first-rate performance.' It was said so quietly Sarah barely caught it, trying to suppress her feeling of surprise at Ben's praise, although logically there was no reason why she should feel surprised. Ben was quite right, it had been a first-rate performance, the credit, she suspected, as much due to the director as to the cast. Dale was extremely proud of his rogue male image, and could surely only have been persuaded to accept the role because of the film's box office potential.

'I'm going to get cleaned up,' exclaimed the actor who was playing Richard's lover. Sarah recognised him from a tough spy series she had seen on television and suppressed a small smile as she heard him to say to Dale, 'I don't know about you, but the only way I'm able to play this is by telling myself you're a delectable female, dressed up in male clothing!'

General laughter greeted the comment, and the group round the set started to disperse.

'Want a ride back with me?'

Sarah jumped. She hadn't seen Dale approaching and was just about to reply when a shadow darkened her vision, Ben's fingers curling painfully round her upper arm.

'No need,' he informed Dale coolly. 'She's coming back with me, aren't you, darling?' Before Sarah could retreat he bent his head. Her lips parted on a startled cry of panic as his fingers snapped round her wrists, pinning them to her sides. With a callous lack of concern for her feelings, Ben's mouth closed over hers. Time swung back leaving Sarah dizzily suspended in space, a helpless groan smothered in her throat as his fingers left her wrist to circle it; stroking, caressing, his mouth leaving her lips to find the hidden susceptible spot behind her ear.

Her breathing ragged, Sarah tried to pull away, her voice slurred and unsteady as she begged him to let her go.

'Kiss me,' Ben ordered thickly against her throat, his fingers stroking along its vulnerable length, and Sarah knew with a sickening sense of unreality that he wouldn't let her go until she obeyed; and worse—that the reason for his command was to humiliate her in front of Dale. Closing her eyes, she tried to force her trembling lips to keep still, her body stiffly unyielding as she forced her mouth to brush Ben's fleetingly. His

hand tightened in her hair, his fingers spread
against the back of her head, forcing her mouth to
remain in contact with his, his mocking, 'If that's
the best you can do, you're no actress,' whispered
against her skin and making her retort savagely, 'I
loathe the feel of you so much I *can't* act!'
invoking first a muttered curse, and then not the
cruel embrace she had tensed herself against but
instead, the sensual brush of his tongue over the
outline of her closed lips, again and again until her
senses stirred in spite of herself and her mouth
parted on a husky moan,

'Say again that you loathe me—if you dare,'
Ben murmured triumphantly, lifting his head to
scrutinise her softly flushed face and betrayingly
languorous eyes.

'What a pity Dale didn't stay to see how much
you loathe me,' Ben taunted sardonically as he
released her. 'Perhaps then he'd appreciate how I
felt when I found the two of you together—you in
his arms, not three days after you had promised
yourself to me.'

'What are you doing, Ben?' Sarah demanded
tiredly, pulling away from him, unaware of the
defeated droop of her neck, or the brilliant
disorder of her hair, cascading round her
shoulders as she turned away from him. 'Keeping
your hand in as an actor? Pity there's no
appreciative audience. I'm tired,' she added wanly.
'I'd like to get back to the site. If you don't want
to take me I'll go as I came, with Lois.'

'I'll take you,' Ben informed her grittily. 'Go
and collect your hat and we'll leave.'

While Ben had been kissing her, stamping her

irrevocably as his property, Sarah thought bitterly, everyone else had moved tactfully away; the camera crew were dismantling their equipment, people making a general move towards packing up, and it was plain that filming was over for the day.

'Ben darling, how much longer are you going to be?'

'Gina, you'll have to find someone else to take you back, Sarah and I are going into town.'

Sarah turned and saw Gina Frey pouting sulkily at Ben, but it was on Sarah that her eyes rested, and the animosity in them was unmistakable.

'I thought town was barred to the cast and crew,' she said acidly.

'So it is, but you must allow me to bend the rules a little in my own favour. Sarah and I have only recently been reconciled.' Sarah wasn't aware that Ben had reached for her hand until he raised it to his lips, turning it palm upwards and touching the softly sensitive skin there with the tip of his tongue. It was impossible to stop the response rippling through her. That Gina was as aware of it as Ben, she couldn't doubt. The other woman's dark eyes narrowed and then flashed bitterly. 'I'm taking Sarah out to dinner.'

It was obvious to Sarah that Gina wanted to object, and equally plain that there was little she could say. However, Gina obviously wasn't easily thrown.

'R.J. will be phoning me later,' she purred felinely. 'He keeps asking how the filming's going. He's getting most anxious about his investment, poor darling.' Eyes narrowed, teeth gleaming against the red gloss of her lips, she eyed Ben triumphantly, her meaning quite plain! 'Play along with me or I'll cause trouble with one of the backers,' and Sarah waited tensely to see how Ben would respond.

'I think you'll find he's feeling much happier now,' Ben told her expressionlessly. 'I spoke to him this morning to tell him that the camera was fixed and that we should be able to make some progress. In fact, I've invited him out here so that he can see for himself how we spend our backers' money.'

A low hiss as she expelled her breath was Gina's only response before she turned and stormed angrily away.

'Phew!' Ben shook his head rather like a diver emerging from the surf, a wicked grin tugging at the corners of his mouth. Seen like that he looked years younger, but the familiar tug on her heartstrings warned Sarah that she would be a fool to forget what he really was. He had undermined her defences dangerously easily already. She mustn't let it happen again. 'Now, your hat, and then we'll be on our way. We're dining with some friends of mine.'

'We are?' Sarah stared at him. 'But you said nothing to me before! I can't go out to dinner dressed like this!' Infuriated with herself, she stared up at him. What she had intended to say was that she wouldn't go out to dinner with him full stop. 'And I don't have a hat,' she added petulantly. 'I forgot to buy one. I'll get one tomorrow.'

'Indeed you will,' Ben agreed grittily. 'You crazy

little fool, do you know what the temperature is out here?' He gestured around him, indicating the exposed and burning half-desert plain. 'And you with that pale Celtic skin and God alone knows how little resistance to the sun!'

'Don't worry, I covered myself liberally with sunscreen before I came out,' Sarah told him acidly. 'I'm not a complete fool, Ben, I do realise that you won't want me looking like a freshly boiled lobster.'

'Correct me if I'm wrong, but to the best of my knowledge they haven't as yet invented a sunscreen that can be applied to the head, right?' Ben demanded, teeth snapping together over the final word. 'Have you no sense, Sarah?' he demanded huskily, raking irate fingers through his hair. 'And as for not being suitably dressed for dinner,' he added, not waiting for an answer, 'that can soon be remedied. I could do with a shower myself, but I've had enough of Gina for one day without having to endure her company on the ride back to the site.'

'You really don't like her, do you?' Sarah asked, surprised into the question by his grim expression.

'She's a man-eater, and not even a subtle one at that. You know me, Sarah,' he mocked, watching her colour come and go as his eyes moved slowly over her jean-clad legs and upwards, resting momentarily on the soft thrust of her breasts against the cotton of her blouse. 'At heart I'm a hunter . . .'

'A hunter who enjoys maiming and wounding his prey,' Sarah agreed bitterly. 'Yes, I know you, Ben.'

'Then you'll know I mean what I say when I tell you that if you so much as let any member of the cast or crew even suspect that we're not the happily reunited lovers I've told them we are, then I'll make you sorry you were ever born!'

'Again?' Sarah drawled with fine irony, watching his face darken with the swift tide of colour running up under his skin, his fingers clenching as though he would dearly like to fasten them round her throat. 'How very boring!'

'Oh, I don't think you'll think so,' Ben assured her tautly. 'Hell can come in many different guises.'

And as she shivered under the impact of the implied threat Sarah cursed bitterly at the whim of fate that had brought them together again. She could, if she was completely impartial and logical, accept why Ben would not want the rest of the crew and cast to think she was having an affair with Dale; she could even by stretching that logic and impartiality to its fullest extent appreciate why he had taken the steps he had to make sure they would not, but this . . . this constant tormenting of her nerves; the subtle sexual pressure he was exerting; these were things she could not understand, and they unnerved her, completely undermining the self-confidence she had built up after their break-up.

'I think I'll just go over and check tomorrow's schedule,' Sarah announced as Ben unlocked the trailer door. 'I should be back by the time you've had your shower.'

'Make sure you are,' Ben warned her. 'Don't

make me come looking for you, Sarah.'

The bar by the pool was crowded, as was the restaurant. Lois called out a greeting as Sarah walked past. She was seated with some of the camera crew who acknowledged her as well. 'Nothing for you tomorrow apart from wardrobe,' Lois called to her, obviously anticipating where she was going. 'Want to join us?'

'I can't, I'm afraid. Ben's taking me out to dinner.' Sarah didn't realise how intimate the words sounded until they were uttered, but Lois, irrepressible as ever, joked:

'To judge from the way he was behaving this afternoon I thought you *were* his dinner, or was that just an appetiser?'

Her cheeks stinging with colour, Sarah made some inarticulate response. She knew that Lois meant well, but her comment had reminded her uncomfortably of how she hadn't been able to stop herself from responding to Ben's touch. She started to shake, memories rolling over her, swamping her.

'Sarah, are you all right? You're so pale. Aren't you feeling well?'

The concern in Dale's voice, the caring touch of his hand on her arm, were instantly soothing.

'It's nothing,' she assured him huskily, glad of his sudden appearance. 'I just felt slightly sick.'

'I'm not surprised, after that display Ben gave this afternoon. You know what it's all about, of course? He's using you to keep Gina at bay,' Dale told her before she could respond. 'He hopes that by producing a "wife", he'll be able to hold off

Gina and still keep R.J. as a backer. He always was a quick thinker, I'll give him that. Be careful, Sarah, that you don't get in deeper than you expect. If I know Ben he won't be averse to doing everything he can to make your "reconciliation" look viable.' His eyes dropped to her hand, which he was now holding lightly within his own. 'I'm no angel myself, but unlike Ben I like my sex sweetened with at least some emotion. He's a cold devil, Sarah. He always was.'

'You can't be trying to warn me that Ben might want to . . . to . . . make love to me,' she got out at last, trembling over the words, guiltily aware that the response of her body to them wasn't entirely one of revulsion.

'You'd better believe it,' Dale told her grimly. 'He wants you, Sarah, I saw it in his eyes this afternoon.'

'No . . . No, I'm sure you're wrong.' Why did her voice sound so breathless? 'I . . .'

'He wants you,' Dale pressed bitterly. 'He wants you because he thinks he'll be taking you away from me. He never was a good loser.'

With a small cry Sarah pulled away from him. Not now—dear God, not now! She didn't *want* to be reminded of the past; of the wager which had caused her so much pain; the pain that lived inside her still; eating at her, destroying her faith in men, her ability to give her love and herself to any man, still hurting from the wounds inflicted by Ben's duplicity and coldhearted seduction of her. He had blinded her with false words of love and even falser promises for the future, and like a fool she had believed him.   Without being aware of it her feet had carried her back to the trailer. The sun was setting, a crimson ball of fire dying into clouds of purple and amber, and she paused to watch, an odd lump in her throat, reluctant to walk into the trailer and yet fearful of the consequences if she did not.

Her fingers were on the handle when it turned against her and the door was thrust open. Ben stood in the aperture, a towel knotted carelessly round his hips, moisture gleaming on his skin. Had his body always been so overpoweringly male? Sarah shuddered, unable to draw her eyes away, conscious of the trembling reaction in her stomach.

'I thought you were going to stand there all night. You always were one for putting off the evil moment, weren't you, Sarah? Remember how you didn't want to do that scene for *Shakespeare*? The one where I finally got to take you to bed?' he added cruelly, watching the colour run up under her skin with detached amusement. 'I suppose that's why you married me before deciding you wanted Dale. How long did he stay with you? What's the matter?' he asked softly. 'You're trembling like a virgin who's never seen a man before,' his mouth mocked her, 'and we both know you're not that, don't we, Sarah?' he said slowly, watching the hot colour consume her pale skin. 'Oh, come, surely it can't have been as memorable as all that? Not when you've got Dale to remember as well.'

'That's . . .' That's not true, she had been about to say, but those words could never be uttered. Better that he think her a wanton than a fool. 'That's a vile thing to say,' she finished weakly.

'So it was,' Ben agreed blandly, his expression changing as he added acidly, 'and an even viler thing to do, wouldn't you say? You'd better get changed,' he told her, changing the subject, like a predator suddenly tiring of tormenting its prey. 'The couple we're dining with are Spaniards—so you can err on the side of formality. And take a coat. My car is parked in the compound and they've been forecasting rain for the last couple of days. That's why it's so hot. Fortunately it won't affect the filming.'

'Ben . . .' Her voice sounded thick with tears even in her own ears, and she wanted to cringe beneath the look he gave her.

'Couldn't we . . . couldn't we call a truce for the duration of the film?' she pleaded weakly. She couldn't go on like this, fencing with him, unable to defend herself from his expert thrusts. Already she felt as though she were bleeding from a thousand tiny cuts.

'A truce?' Ben laughed harshly. 'Oh no, Sarah, that isn't what I have in mind at all. The bathroom's all yours,' he called over his shoulder as he went back inside. 'We could have shared it, but then you always were something of a prude. Perhaps Dale's managed to coax you out of it.'

A prude! Sarah felt as though he had stuck a knife straight into her heart. She had been shy and inexperienced, yes, but surely no man could describe the complete and utter abandonment she had experienced in Ben's arms as prudish?

'That's something you'll never find out,' she managed to throw at him as she followed him into the trailer, forgetting in her determination to retaliate that her words might be taken as a challenge.

She didn't relax until he was in his room, and all the time she was showering, despite the locked door between them, she felt strung up and on edge, her fingers clumsy as she donned fresh underwear, and pulled on a silk dress in her favourite shade of lavender grey. It was a hot, sultry night and she was careful to apply only the minimum of make-up. She saw Ben studying her when she emerged from her room and asked defensively, 'Is something wrong?'

'Not as far as I'm concerned, I'm just wondering how far your appearance is going to go to reinforcing our host's belief that all film actresses wear skin-tight dresses with slit skirts and have brass-blonde hair. He's rather old-fashioned,' he added lightly. 'You should have a lot in common. Tell me something that's always puzzled me, Sarah—how did you manage to salve your puritan conscience when you took Dale for your lover? Or did you love him so much conscience never came into it?'

'I ... I don't want to talk about it,' she managed desperately. 'The past is over, Ben. I don't want to remember any of it.'

'I bet you damn well don't! I wish to God I could forget as easily,' he snarled, frightening her with the rage she saw in his eyes as he threw open the door. The soft silk of his shirt sleeve brushed her bare arm as he stood back for her to pass, and instantly an electric awareness of him pulsed through her. It was no good, she thought dizzily, trying to regain control of her thudding pulses. Nothing had changed. She loved him still, foolishly, crazily in view of all that had happened, but quite, quite irrevocably.

CHAPTER FOUR

'YOUR friends live here?' Sarah stared aghast at the impressive villa with its private drive.

'I got to know them when I came out to do some preliminary work on ... on the locations. The family once owned the castle we're using for some of the shots. Now most of their wealth comes from sherry. There's no need to be nervous.'

'I'm not,' Sarah flashed back, angry that he had seen through her defences, conscious that she was lying and of a sense of trepidation about facing Ben's friends. 'Do they ... do they know you're bringing me with you? That we're married?' she questioned dry-mouthed. What had Ben told them about her?

'Yes, and yes, but you needn't worry that you'll be asked any awkward questions. I've simply told them that we'd had problems but that we've now reconciled them.'

'And later,' Sarah found herself asking tautly, 'when all this is over, what will you tell them then?'

'Does it matter? I'll think of something.' Ben was getting out of the car, coming round to her door and opening it for her, his hand touching her arm impersonally as he helped her out, and she found she was shivering despite the heat pressing down on her like a heavy blanket, her teeth almost chattering as she flung at him:

'Of course you will. You're good at that, aren't

you, Ben? Always quick to turn a situation to your own advantage.'

'Meaning what?' he demanded icily, gripping her arm and swinging her round to face him. Heavy cloud blanketed the stars and moon and it was impossible for her to see his face, but she could feel the tautly suppressed anger coming off his body.

'Meaning what, Sarah?' he reiterated harshly. 'Snide little innuendoes are one thing, aren't they? Actually being able to validate them is something else again.'

The scorn in his voice lashed at her pride. She *wouldn't* just stand there and let him tear her to pieces! 'Meaning that you've used me and our marriage to keep Gina at bay, just as you used me once before to . . .' She couldn't go on, her voice totally suspended, she could only shake her head weakly, unable to put into words how she had felt when Dale told her about their bet.

'Oh, I see!' She felt him take a step towards her and shrank back against the car instinctively, shuddering as the clouds parted momentarily and a silvered beam revealed his features to her quite distinctly. His eyes were hard and cold, his mouth grimly sardonic, contempt and mockery dominating his expression. 'You worked that out all by yourself, did you?'

'No!' Goaded, Sarah defended herself instantly. He wasn't going to accuse her of simply imagining things. 'Dale . . .'

'Ah yes, Dale,' Ben broke in dangerously, not giving her the chance to continue. 'I thought he'd figure somewhere in this. Dale told you I was

using you to keep Gina at bay, did he, Sarah? *Did*
he, Sarah?' he demanded savagely, his fingers
closing on her wrist so painfully that she cried out.

'You're hurting me!' she protested huskily,

'Not half as much as I'd like to,' was his brutal
retort. 'How it must gall Dale to know that I had
you first!'

The crudity of his comment and the savage
satisfaction in the way he voiced it held her silent
for a handful of seconds, all ability to respond
suspended by the ferocity of the pain invading her.

'Not half as much as it does me,' she told him
quietly, when she was able. 'Ben, I don't think
tonight's a good idea, I . . .'

'Too late,' he mocked her, 'we've been seen.' He
gestured towards the front door which was being
opened, and then he leaned forward suddenly,
capturing her lips, the pressure of his mouth hard
and sure, his head lifting almost immediately.
'There,' he drawled, stopping her as she opened
her handbag to reach for her lipstick. 'No, leave
it,' he ordered, taking the tube from her and
dropping it back into her bag, snapping it shut.

'But they'll know you've been kissing me,' Sarah
protested, not understanding.

'So they will,' Ben agreed laconically, 'which is
better than having them think I've been quarrelling
with you, wouldn't you agree?'

'And so you're playing Joanna?'

Sarah nodded her head. The Sarjoves were a
pleasant couple, Miguel Sarjoves a South American
by birth who had married Luisa when she was
visiting his country with her aunt. As Luisa had

had no brothers, and he himself was a younger son, he had returned to Spain with her, managing her share of the family sherry business. They had two daughters and a son, Luisa had told her over dinner, all of whom were away at school. Now they were seated in the handsome drawing room drinking coffee, and Luisa was questioning Sarah about her role in the film.

'It's a marvellous part,' Sarah enthused. 'I can't get over how lucky I am to have got it.'

'Oh, but surely,' Luisa began, glancing at Ben, 'as . . .'

'I didn't give Sarah the part,' Ben interrupted easily. 'Guy did that.'

'Yes, mainly because my colouring was so right,' Sarah informed her.

'We had no idea that Ben was married until he told us about you,' Luisa admitted. 'He stayed with us for several months and I thought at the time that there was something troubling him, some problem . . .'

'He was probably worrying about how much filming would have to be done on location and how much it was going to cost,' Sarah told her dryly, knowing quite well that whatever Ben had been worried about, it couldn't have been her.

Luisa was regarding her oddly, her eyes going to Ben's shuttered face and then back again. 'Oh, but I meant when he was . . .'

'Sarah, if you're ready, I think it's time we were making a move,' Ben interrupted lazily. 'Filming starts at six tomorrow—one of the battle scenes— and apart from the fact that the light will be better, even with modern techniques, chain mail still weighs heavy. There's a limit to the time one can expect the cast to wear it in this heat!'

The drive back to the site was accomplished without incident. Sarah's head had started to ache during the meal and she had put it down to the fact that she wasn't used to dining so late, plus the richness of the food and wine, and she had been glad that Ben had left her in peace.

The storm still had not broken, and the night was oppressive as she slid from the car, leaving Ben to lock it as she walked towards the trailer. He caught up with her just as she drew level with the pool area and it was obvious from the activity round the bar that some people were not too concerned with getting up early in the morning.

'Hey, boss, come and have a drink with us,' someone called out, but Ben shook his head, cupping Sarah's elbow, his refusal giving rise to several witticisms that brought a film of colour to Sarah's face.

They entered the trailer in silence, and Ben went straight to the living area and opened a cupboard, producing a bottle and a glass. Sarah frowned as she watched him pour some of the fiery spirit into the tumbler, wondering a little that he should want it after what they had eaten and drunk with their hosts.

'I think I'll go to bed, if you don't mind,' she heard herself saying, recognising the edge of tension in her voice.

'How polite we are!' Ben jeered as he picked up the glass. 'Pity you didn't ask me if I'd any objections before you took Dale for your lover.'

In the bathroom Sarah showered quickly, dreading the moment when she would have to emerge from its sanctuary dressed only in her nightdress and thin robe, but when she did Ben never raised his head from the paperwork spread out over the table. He had switched off all the lights apart from a powerful lamp which threw into relief the angled planes of his face, distorting them slightly so that Sarah could almost deceive herself that she saw vulnerability and pain etched against the darkness of his skin. He had always tanned easily. She remembered when they were filming *Shakespeare* there had been a particularly hot spell and he had been lazily amused by the contrast in the colour and texture of their bodies. When he had made love to her it had been almost as though his skin transferred the heat and molten power of the sun to hers, burning her more tender flesh with the contact. How magical that night had seemed! He had taken her out to dinner and throughout the meal all she could think of was how she had felt when he held her against him that day during the filming. He had glanced up and caught her eyes on the exposed vee of flesh at his throat, and with a sudden imprecation he had grasped her hand, reaction shivering across her skin as he muttered her name huskily.

After that she had only toyed with her meal. He had driven her back to her lodgings, turning to her in the darkness of his car, kissing her with a hunger that swept aside all her fears and reservations. She had played Mary Fitton for so long that her body had become pliantly responsive to his, responding instantly to the stroke of his thumb over the tautness of her breast. When he bent his head to its burgeoning arousal she had had a momentary detached image of its darkness against the paleness of her skin before the dark floodtide of desire closed swirlingly over her. She couldn't remember what Ben had said when he finally released her, only the brief drive to his flat, the silence thick with his unspoken intent. In his bedroom she had trembled eagerly against him when he touched her, wanting his total possession of her with a need that pushed aside the barriers of prudence and inexperience.

Afterwards he had been full of remorse, or so it had seemed, teasing her a little over her panic that others might guess they had been lovers, demanding to know if she was ashamed of their relationship, but she hadn't been able to explain her dread of the knowing eyes of the rest of the cast, the laughter and comments that would follow, not realising until later, when she saw the first rushes, that she had already betrayed herself and that her love for Ben was there for all to see in the incandescence of their love scenes.

Of course, she hadn't realised then why he wanted their affair to become public knowledge; hadn't known a thing about his bet with Dale. That had come after he had been forced to take the almost unbelievable step of marrying her. 'Oh, Ben's like that in pursuit of his goal,' Dale had told her carelessly when she refused to accept that he would go so far simply to win a wager. 'Single-minded isn't the word. Besides, making you fall in love with him has a double advantage. One, he gets to win the bet, and two, it comes across so obviously on film, and gives his performance the edge over mine. You don't know him like I do, Sarah,' he had told her. 'We went through drama school together. I've seen him in action before.' And because she had doubted all along that Ben could actually love her, and because she knew Dale had no axe to grind, Sarah had been forced to accept that he was right.

She slept fitfully, missing the open window she always insisted on at home, but knowing that the heat outside would quickly negate the cooling effect of the air-conditioning if she did open one. Her headache grew progressively worse, nausea adding to her misery. There was a medicine cabinet in the bathroom, with luck with some aspirin in it, and she swung her feet out of the bed, surprised to discover that she was shivering with cold, despite the clammy stickiness of her skin. When she opened the door, the brief staccato noise of the typewriter startled her. It was gone two in the morning; what was Ben doing typing, and why?

Whatever he was doing was totally engrossing; his head turned to one side away from her as he studied something beside him, her presence unnoticed as she crept into the bathroom. Without sleep to fog her brain she was unpleasantly aware that her 'symptoms' could easily be those of sunstroke, and she could only pray that it was only a mild dose and that she would be fully recovered by morning. Just as soon as she had seen Wardrobe she *must* get herself a hat!

Unwilling to draw Ben's attention to herself, she

resisted the desire to switch on the bathroom light and instead felt her way towards the medicine cupboard, her eyes adjusting themselves to the lack of light enough for her to get it open. There were several bottles inside, any of which might contain what she wanted. Giving an exasperated sigh as much at her own folly as anything else, she reached for one, intending to hold it up to the light of the window, but somehow it slipped from her fingers, crashing down into the basin below, showering her with fragments of glass as it splintered, and leaving her transfixed with shock.

She heard Ben curse fluently, the trailer illuminated with light as he moved, switching lights on, thrusting open the bathroom door to stare at her in mingled anger and scorn.

'I had a headache ... I saw you were working and didn't want to disturb you ...' Heavens, she sounded like a terrified child, Sarah thought mentally, suddenly intensely conscious of the fact that his silk shirt was open almost to the waist, exposing tanned flesh, darkened by a fine covering of hair. Instantly she was aware of her body's response; the provocative firming of her breasts, imperfectly concealed by her thin cotton nightdress, and she made to take a step forward, desperate to escape the close confines of the small room, dominated by Ben's masculinity and her reaction to it, even the air so thick with tension that she could barely breathe.

'Sarah, no!' The whiplash command cut through her thoughts. She paused, heard Ben swear, and the next moment he was crunching through the broken glass to swing her into his arms.

'What's the matter with you?' he demanded furiously. 'Do you want to cut your feet to ribbons?'

She had completely forgotten the broken glass and shuddered violently as she looked down at it.

'You're cold!'

To her surprise there was concern in his voice. Still holding her in his arms, he carried her through into the living area, barely half a dozen strides in all, but more than enough to make her uncomfortably aware of the suppleness and strength of sinews and bone covered by skin that gleamed like oiled silk. Before he put her down Ben steadied himself against the door, the movement catching her off guard and making her clutch at his shirt, the skin beneath it vibrantly warm and slightly damp with the perspiration she could see clinging to the pores of his face. Was it really so warm? She shivered convulsively as he put her down, unaware of the material of her nightdress tightening across her breasts until she realised that Ben was looking at her, his body slightly tensed. From being cold Sarah suddenly felt as though she were consumed by a burning heat. It seared her skin, drying out her mouth, her breathing suddenly forced and uneven. She touched her tongue to her dry lips, wanting to break the silence that stretched between them taut as fine wire and yet at the same time strangely unwilling to break the spell it wove.

Like someone in a dream she saw Ben's hand come up, slowly, as though he were moving through water, his thumb brushing the erect peak of her nipple, his eyes darkening to onyx as he bent over her, tugging at the ribbons securing the bodice of her nightdress, his fingers unbelievably gentle as they cupped the swollen flesh he had exposed.

He made a brief sound, swiftly checked as Sarah's gaze flew to his face, familiar and yet oddly unfamiliar as he looked down at her, an expression in his eyes that made her catch her breath quiveringly, panting slightly as he bent his head and slowly touched his lips to the place where his thumb had lingered.

Pain and pleasure seared through her together as Sarah closed her eyes, not knowing which of them had made the faint sound of satisfaction, oblivious to everything but a compelling desire to weave her fingers into the fine black silk of Ben's hair and hold him against her breast. She moved towards him, jarring her arm against the table, and the impact filled the small space with alien sounds. Ben's brilliant unfocused gaze left her body, his features hardening as they swept her face and she was thrust from him.

'Go back to bed, Sarah,' he told her hardily. 'I'm in no mood tonight to play stand-in for Dale.'

It shattered her mood instantaneously, and it wasn't until she was on her feet that she remembered the shattered glass in the bathroom, and the aspirin she still hadn't got. Well, Ben could clear up the broken glass, she told herself, childishly, and as for the aspirin—after what had just happened she doubted if a whole bottleful would be sufficient to make her sleep. Her body trembled with nervous tension, every nerve ending still raw with the ache Ben's touch had evoked, and she knew shamingly that if he were to come to her now she would be dangerously close to begging him to make love to her. However, she wasn't entirely a fool—not nowadays—and she didn't waste time delving into the reasons behind Ben's actions. They had been pure reflex, an entirely impersonal reaction of any male who suddenly became aware that he was holding a half-naked female in his arms.

She supposed it was only to be expected that she should wake up heavy-eyed, with her head throbbing and her stomach still queasy, Sarah decided as she crawled out of bed, reaching for her robe. A glance at her watch showed that it was just after eight. Fortunately her wardrobe call wasn't until ten, and at least she would have the trailer to herself.

There was no sign of any broken glass in the bathroom. Ben had made some attempt to tidy away his papers in the living area, although one had drifted down on to the floor. She bent to pick it up automatically, glancing at the typewritten page, her brows drawing together in a frown as she read it. It was obviously a page of typescript, but just as obviously it had nothing to do with their present film. Perhaps Ben was already looking for his next film, that wouldn't be entirely unheard-of, but there were several mistakes in the typing, and what she was holding was a carbon copy rather than an original, the typescript looking as though it could belong to Ben's rather battered manual machine. Telling herself that she was becoming dangerously obsessive about him, Sarah placed the paper on the table and set about making herself a cup of coffee. The thought of food made her feel faintly ill, and she noticed as she glanced through the window that the sky was unpleasantly sullen, the sun shining brassily down on the hard-baked earth.

By nine-thirty she had re-read her lines and was ready for her wardrobe appointment. Afterwards she would seek out Lois or one of the other girls and find out where she could best get transport to take her into town. Today she must get a hat. She was nearly sure that her headache and nausea were the result of too much exposure to the sun, and today, if anything, it was even hotter.

The wardrobe mistress, Linda Dawes, was a slim blonde girl with a businesslike manner, who measured Sarah quickly and then complimented her on the factuality of her data sheet. 'You wouldn't believe the number of actresses, and actors come to that, who tell us they're inches thinner than they actually are, and we're supposed to make their costumes! I must be lucky this time out, both you and Eva Martell who's playing Eleanor measure out exactly right. She's got an appointment this morning too, which means I'll probably be able to finish early enough to have a dip in the pool. Stifling outside, isn't it?'

Sarah agreed. 'And I've got to find something to drive into town later. I have to get a hat,' she explained. 'Unless you've got something?'

Linda shook her head. 'Sorry, I haven't, but I can lend you my car. It's not exactly in the first flush of youth.' She looked doubtfully at Sarah, but she was too grateful for the offer to reject it.

'It's an old Mini, I'll give you the keys later. It's parked in the compound and you can't miss it. It's bright yellow.'

As she worked Sarah discovered that Linda was English like herself, but that she had worked in Hollywood for several years. 'There's so much more scope over there,' she told Sarah. 'We've designed these costumes to complement your colouring,' she explained, as she produced several silky tunics in rich greens and blues. 'Nothing too subtle—they simply didn't have the means of dyeing them, although we can go to town a bit more later in the film—once you're married to William of Sicily. Messina was an international port and it's feasible that silks and fabrics from the East would find their way there. In particular I thought you ought to wear something gauzy and provocative for your meeting with de Courcy, when he comes to tell you that Richard has managed to secure your dowry. You loved him as a girl, now you're a widow—a woman—and you want him to be aware of the fact. You married as you had to—a man of fifty, impotent and gross, and now you feel you've earned the right to love, and you do still love him, and since you are a queen and he is merely a knight you have to show him that love.'

'By dressing in Eastern silks?' Sarah teased, but she could tell that Linda was completely absorbed in her job.

'What do you think of the script?' Linda asked her, her mouth half full of pins as she slipped the first of the costumes over Sarah's head.

'It's fantastic. I only wish there was a chance of

meeting the author. I thought he might be here—on site—you know they sometimes are.'

'Umm.' Linda frowned, studying the fall of the fabric. 'You know it's rumoured that...' She broke off as the trailer door opened and a tall elegant woman in her late forties entered, apologising as she saw Sarah. 'I'm sorry, I know I'm a little early.'

'We're nearly through,' Linda assured her. 'Like you, Sarah was strictly accurate with her measurements—thank God. Do you two know one another, Eva?' she asked the older woman.

'Only slightly,' Eva Martell replied, smiling at Sarah. 'We worked together briefly on *Shakespeare*, I don't know if you remember?'

'Yes, I do,' Sarah confirmed warmly. The older woman had had a small part, sandwiched in between other work in America, but Sarah could still remember how kind she had been to a raw young girl fresh out of drama school.

'And now you and Ben are back together. I'm glad. He went through a bad time after you left him, and of course Dale's gloating didn't help, but they say that's Dale all over. He's always been jealous of Ben. Of course he's a first-rate actor, but he doesn't have Ben's talent for diversification. Even when they were at drama school together it was obvious that Ben would never simply be content to act.'

It was plain to Sarah that nothing she could say could correct the older woman's erroneous impressions, and she wondered a little cynically what Eva's response would be were she to tell her the true facts surrounding her relationship with and marriage to Ben. Dale jealous of Ben! Why, it was ridiculous. Dale had known right from the start that all she felt for him was brotherly affection, an affection which she knew he returned—witness the way he had allowed her to use him to protect her pride, letting Ben think they were lovers.

'Hey, don't forget these,' Linda called after her as she finished dressing and walked towards the trailer door. 'My car keys,' she explained when Sarah looked blank. 'You wanted to go into town?'

Thanking her for reminding her, Sarah said goodbye to Eva and left the trailer.

If anything the heat had intensified. The short walk from Linda's trailer to Ben's was enough to make her feel sick and shaky, her head tender to the harsh brilliance of the sun. Once inside, she gulped thankfully at the cool air, nauseated by the thought of lunch and settling instead for some fresh orange juice she found in the fridge. She must come to some arrangement with Ben over the cost of her keep. The fridge and freezer were well stocked and she suspected he probably ordered food weekly from the stores. She would check at the shop later in the day when she replaced the juice she had drunk—and she had better get some aspirins. She was glad there was no one to see the way her face flamed painfully as she remembered the way Ben had watched and touched her, almost as though he hadn't been able to stop himself. She was being stupid, she chided herself, allowing her imagination to colour reality with her own desires. Never at any time, apart from the night they had made love, had Ben given any indication of not being wholly in control of his reactions, and even that night had been a sham; a deliberate intent to seduce her. For making love to her she could forgive him, but for allowing her to believe that he had done so in love, she could not. Quickly rinsing her glass, she found her handbag, checked that she had money and traveller's cheques, and before the weight of her thoughts became too much for her, left the trailer.

Linda had been right when she described her car as 'ancient', Sarah reflected, as the small vehicle ploughed through the dust of the main road, but at least with such a variety of odd sounds and rattles to choose from, she wasn't going to worry about a particular one.

It took longer to reach the small town she had passed through with Dale than she expected, but then she had been travelling in the luxury of Dale's expensive sports car. A small smile tugged at her lips. Dale had always had a little-boy need for the trappings of fame; unlike Ben who she remembered had driven an ordinary saloon car when they were filming *Shakespeare*, although she had to admit the BMW he had been driving the previous evening had been considerably more luxurious.

CHAPTER FIVE

PARKING her car under the shade of one of the trees in the town's small, dusty square, Sarah climbed out and looked uncertainly around her. The square was empty and quiet—too quiet, she realised, noticing the shuttered and silent appearance of the buildings bordering it, and then it struck her! She was in Spain, not England, and it was siesta time! The headache which had been plaguing her all morning returned, the agonising throbbing in her temples increasing as she tried to think. It was barely gone lunchtime, which meant that it could be several hours before the shops reopened. What should she do? She couldn't even see a café where she could sit and wait. This was no holiday town geared to the odd ways of *turistas*, she probably wouldn't even be able to *find* a hat when the shops did open, she reflected forlornly, wishing she had given a little more thought to her mission before setting out. There wasn't even a chemist's shop open where she might have been able to buy something to relieve her headache and nausea.

She shivered suddenly. How silent the square was, the air oppressive, the sultry glare of the sun almost menacing. As she glanced at the horizon she saw the thick pall of cloud, presaging the storm Ben had mentioned. She had no alternative but to return to the site. At least if there was a storm, she comforted herself, it would negate the risk of her suffering from fresh sunstroke. She recollected that there had been a shop selling sunhats at the airport, and if the worst came to the worst she could always go there tomorrow; she wasn't needed for filming for another day. Trying to uplift her depressed spirits by this reasoning, she headed back to the car. Nothing seemed to have gone right since she arrived in Spain, and she had been so looking forward to it; so excited when she saw Dale waiting for her outside the airport building. Dale . . . she bit her lip as she got into the car. How sweet and understanding he was! Never once had he taken her to task for lying to him about her divorce. She frowned a little, wondering why he had *not* mentioned it, especially as he must have found it embarrassing to learn the truth from Ben rather than from her. How Ben must have gloated to be able to throw that 'ex-wife' back in his face! She frowned, her hands stilling, the scene coming unbidden to the surface of her mind in a series of sharply clear pictures. Dale, tossing the casual words at Ben. Ben, grim-faced, relentless, Dale, smiling mockingly, *Dale* . . . gloating?

Sarah shied away from the image. How ridiculous she was being! Dale had had nothing to gloat about, the words had simply slipped from his tongue accidentally; meant at worst as a lightly teasing comment. She was letting her foolish love for Ben play on her imagination, she thought shakily as she started the car. Dale was the one who had protected her from Ben's treachery, upholding her pride . . .

She realised as she drove out of the square that

the sun had stopped shining and that the clouds no longer lay massed along the horizon, but instead were threateningly overhead, heavy and ominous. If anything the heat seemed to have increased; not a pleasant heat, but a damply oppressive one, her hands sticky where they clung to the steering-wheel, perspiration beading her temples, her head swimming with pain and nausea.

She heard the thunder as she left the town, the muted rumble in the distance making her automatically increase her speed. She was not particularly frightened of thunderstorms, but this one promised to be extraordinarily spectacular and the effects of the compressed electric energy were making themselves felt on her body. Her skin seemed to burn one minute and then turn to ice the next, her head throbbing agonisingly as she tried to concentrate on her driving. She had only gone half a dozen miles when she felt the small car begin to lose acceleration. Thinking that the loss of power was her own fault, she pressed instinctively on the accelerator, realising with apprehension that the car wasn't responding.

She knew next to nothing about the mechanics of engines, and when the Mini finally coughed to a standstill, for several seconds she could do nothing but sit still in stunned disbelief. What on earth was she going to do? The most sensible course of action open to her was to return to the town. She couldn't remember seeing a garage, but surely there must be one? And a telephone. She would have to phone the site to let them know what had happened to her, although she doubted that she would be missed until Ben returned to the trailer in

the evening. But getting back to the town meant a
walk of six miles. It was a daunting thought,
especially as the first large drops of rain were
already beginning to fall, darkening the road
surface, and splattering noisily on the car's metal
roof.

Perhaps if she simply sat where she was? But she
couldn't help remembering that she had seen no
traffic on the road during her outward journey. As
she had realised when she was in the town, it was
siesta-time, and besides, she wasn't altogether sure
it would be wise to simply hang around waiting for
some knight of the road to offer her a lift.

Rather reluctantly she opened the car door and
eased herself out. She hadn't brought a coat, and
before she had gone much more than a hundred
yards, she was soaked by the heavy rain. The
thunder was nearer now, sheet lightning splitting
open the clouds, and it was still so oppressively
hot! She wouldn't have been entirely surprised to
have seen steam coming off her clothes! Struck by
a fit of giggles, she suddenly realised that she was
feeling quite lightheaded, almost as though her feet
weren't touching the ground. It was an extraordin-
ary sensation, and one that sent alarm bells ringing
in that part of her brain that still held on to
common sense. She was beginning to feel quite
dizzy and faint, and she moistened her suddenly
dry mouth, telling herself that she simply could
not faint, here in the middle of the road during a
thunderstorm. Her eyes felt oddly heavy, her legs
suddenly dangerously wobbly. The road seemed to
shimmer and shiver around her. The sound of a
car, at first a distant hum, grew louder, and she

started to shiver. Dared she risk trying to stop it? The decision was taken out of her hands when she realised it was coming towards her, travelling in the opposite direction from the town, a powerful maroon blur, which took up a good three-quarters of the narrow road, the front wheel hitting a pothole and sending a wave of water cascading over her jeans and thin tee-shirt. Drenched and furious, Sarah wasn't aware that the car had stopped until she heard the faint slam of its door, followed by purposeful footsteps. She turned, her eyes widening in disbelief as she saw her husband coming towards her through the rain, black hair plastered wetly to his skull, the formal suit he was wearing turning him into an imposing stranger. But he *was* a stranger, she thought vaguely as he drew level with her and started to speak, his briefly furious questions reaching her through a barrier of protective fog, the only thing penetrating it his savage exclamation of anger as the drumming in her ears reached crescendo proportions and she slid helplessly to the ground.

When she came round she was sitting in his car. They were motionless on the side of the road, Ben's face decidedly grim as she opened her eyes and found him watching her.

'What the hell's going on?' he demanded bitingly. No words of comfort, no enquiries as to her state of health! Stifling the tears threatening to flow, Sarah tried to sit upright, shivering as she felt the clammy touch of her soaking clothes. 'Well? I'm waiting?'

He could wait until hell froze over as far as she was concerned, Sarah decided crossly, and then seeing the look on his face changed her mind and said quickly, 'I wanted to get myself a hat. Linda, from Costumes, offered to lend me her Mini, but it broke down. I was just walking back to find a garage.'

'You went to buy a hat in the middle of the siesta period? In a town where the women cover their heads with shawls, if they use anything? Have you run completely mad?'

Quivering with anger and humiliation, Sarah turned her head. She *would not* cry, she told herself, biting so hard on her bottom lip that she could taste her blood. She had started to shiver, suddenly desperately cold, unaware of how pale and fragile she looked, her eyes smudged pools of violet in the pallor of her face.

'You were five miles away from the town. Have you any idea of the condition you'd have been in if I hadn't come along when I did?'

Ben was seething, and although in some ways she could understand why her foolishness was infuriating him, she hated knowing that his concern was for the film and the effects any illness of hers might have upon it, rather than for her herself.

'How lucky for me then that you did,' she finally managed in a shakily defiant voice.

'I had to go into Seville. I wanted to send off the rushes from yesterday for myself, and I had some other business to attend to. As you so rightly say, luckily for you. What's the matter?' Ben asked sharply as she shivered again. 'You're not ill, are you?'

If he thought she was ill, he might take her part

away from her, and besides, she wasn't really, Sarah thought hazily. She was just suffering from too much exposure to the sun, or was it too much exposure to Ben that made her feel so weak and trembly?

'I'm wet and cold,' she managed, trying to sound cool and in control. 'I've also got the most dreadful headache.' She saw his mouth compress and realised that she had been unwise, when he gritted, 'You're suffering from heat-stroke, you little fool, and by the looks of it you're trying to compound it by contracting pneumonia as well! You'd better get those wet things off. Here, you can wear this,' he told her carelessly, removing his jacket. 'Once we get going the heater will soon warm the car, but it won't dry out those soaking jeans.'

Even though she knew he was right, she felt a curious reluctance to do as he said. He had seen her in far less than her bra and briefs, she reminded herself as her fingers fumbled with her zip—and as recently as last night. She knew he didn't care a damn about her, and yet she felt ridiculously shy at the thought of removing her clothes.

'Come on, Sarah,' he demanded impatiently. 'I have seen it all before, you know.'

The contempt in his voice opened a still raw wound, reminding her of the look in his eyes, and the—as she had foolishly thought it—reverence in his voice, that night when he had made her his. But that had all been nothing more than a hateful sham.

Averting her head, she slid off her jeans, her

fingers trembling as she tried to tug them free. At her side Ben made a small, explosive sound of impatience, the telling noise jerking her head up so that she could see the tautly implacable line of his jaw. 'Oh, for God's sake,' he muttered, a man goaded beyond the limits of his endurance. 'What are you—a child? Here, let me.' Before she could stop him his brown fingers curled round her ankle and then tugged remorselessly at the heavy, clinging denim. 'And now this,' he continued curtly when her jeans had been tossed into the back seat, and it was useless for her to protest that her tee-shirt was something she could manage quite adequately without his help. The heavy rain had soaked right through the thin fabric and through the soft silk of the bra she was wearing underneath, plastering it to the curves of her breasts, fuller now that she was a woman rather than a girl. For a few brief seconds as he tugged her tee shirt free of her arms, Ben's gaze rested on those curves, and to her utter chagrin and humiliation, Sarah felt them swell and firm, her reaction clearly visible in the burgeoning outline of her nipples against the now taut fabric of her bra. Colour washed her skin in a hot tide, her hands shaking as she shrank back into her seat, pulling on Ben's jacket, expecting with every tension-filled second that passed to hear him making some mocking comment. When he didn't, she risked a glance upwards, feeling happier now that she had the protection of his jacket concealing her body. To her surprise he was staring rigidly out of the window, his skin drawn tightly against the harsh bones of his face, his flesh white where he had compressed his mouth.

'Ready?'

He must have felt her move rather than seen her, because he hadn't so much as spared her a glance. When she gave a rather croaky 'yes', he started the engine, the sound not quite enough to drown out a fresh clap of thunder.

Neither of them spoke, but the silence wasn't an easy one. Sarah felt on edge with the tension of it, the comfort of Ben's jacket fast turning to torture. The fine wool smelled faintly of his cologne, and being wrapped in it was heartbreakingly like being wrapped in Ben's arms, especially when she closed her eyes. At least her headache seemed to have subsided, she thought numbly as they turned off the road and bumped down the track leading to the site.

'I must tell Linda about her car,' she mumbled as Ben drove past the compound and parked outside his trailer.

'Leave it,' he told her curtly. 'I'll see to it. There's a garage in the town—I'll get them to send someone out to it.'

Sarah reached for the door handle, biting back a startled gasp as Ben moved across her, and told her to wait. She closed her eyes as he slid out of the car and came round to her door, opening it quickly and bending to take her in his arms. She started to protest, but he silenced her with a frown, opening the trailer door and carrying her inside, and into her room.

'Stay there,' he commanded briefly as he turned back to the door. 'How are you feeling now?' he asked over his shoulder. 'Faint? Sick?'

'Not as bad as I did,' Sarah responded. 'My head still aches, but that's all.' Even as she spoke she started to shiver, not knowing whether it was reaction to being in Ben's arms or the chilly atmosphere of the trailer. She was reaching up to turn off her air-conditioning unit when Ben came back. He had taken off his shirt and trousers which had got soaked in the short journey from the car to the trailer, and was wearing a towelling robe. Sarah felt her heart pound, her breath catching in her throat as he stood over her frowning. His hair was tousled as though he had been drying it.

'Here, take these,' he instructed her, handing her two capsules. 'I'll get you a glass of water to go with them.'

When he came back she was still shivering. Her whole body felt chilled and she longed for a hot bath, followed by a long sleep. She took the glass he proffered, puzzled but not alarmed when he sat down on the edge of her bed. When she had drunk the water he took the glass from her and picked up a towel. 'Turn round,' he told her coolly. When she looked hesitant, he told her coldly, 'I'm going to dry your hair for you, not rape you. Although it wouldn't be rape, would it, Sarah?' She felt her skin burn at the mocking cynicism she heard in his voice, glad that she had her back to him and that he couldn't see her face.

It was oddly soothing having him rub her hair, his movements brisk but gentle, and she felt as though she could sit there all day—no, not sit there, but lie in his arms, she admitted on a sudden rush of knowledge, her body aching with a sense of rejection as he got up.

When he left without a word she thought he wasn't coming back, but she had just removed his jacket, unable to stop herself from pressing her face against its warmth, when he returned, a fresh towel in his hand, his eyes unreadable as she dropped the jacket as though it had been live coals. Had he seen? He couldn't have done, otherwise surely he would have made some biting comment?

It wasn't until he sat down beside her and calmly unfastened her bra, that Sarah realised he intended to stay. She opened her mouth to protest and found she was being enveloped in a thick, fluffy towel, Ben's hands hard and firm as they rubbed warmth into her chilled skin.

'Ben, I can manage,' she stammered, terrified that he would guess the effect his ministrations were having on her foolishly responsive body, but all he did was raise his eyebrows and comment scathingly:

'Sure you can—the way you were "managing" this afternoon, no doubt. Sit still, Sarah,' he told her, adding drawlingly, 'Who knows? Perhaps you might enjoy it?'

The trouble was *she* did know—that she would! And the knowledge was humiliating. Terrified that he would realise too, she forced herself to keep absolutely still, fighting down the weakly melting tide of desire running hotly through her body when his hand accidentally touched her breast.

'For God's sake relax,' Ben told her. 'What is it? The storm?'

The storm? Sarah had practically forgotten about it, until a particularly loud clap of thunder outside made her jump nervously. No, it was a storm of a different kind she feared—the storm of emotion Ben was arousing by touching her.

'Sarah?' She heard him curse as she stiffened. Simultaneously lightning illuminated the room and she saw her reflection in the mirror, her face white and tense, then Ben was pulling her back against him until her back curved against his chest, his arms locking round her.

'You really are scared, aren't you?' He turned her in his arms, searching her face, and Sarah couldn't deny it. She wasn't just scared; she was petrified. Petrified that if he continued to hold her the way he was doing she would betray herself completely. She hadn't forgotten how a younger Sarah and fought to conceal from him his ultimate victory; that not only had he seduced her body, he had also seduced her heart and mind, and she didn't want him to know it now, either. 'Come on, relax,' Ben told her. 'There's nothing to be afraid of.'

Oh, but there was, Sarah thought yearningly as he pulled her head down against his shoulder. Her body curved into the protection of his, one arm holding her against him while his free hand stroked soothingly over her back. At least it was meant to be soothing, she was sure, only its effect on her was very different. Feelings she had fought to suppress ever since she had seen him boiled up inside her. The shoulder she was pillowed against was hard and warm. The towelling robe had fallen open, revealing his skin sleekly brown over his

collarbone. Quite what came over her afterwards
Sarah wasn't sure, she only knew that she was
impelled by some force greater than her will to
touch her lips to that warm flesh, and then merely
touching it with her lips wasn't enough. Her
fingertips traced the shape of it, her lips following
their course, and she was drowning in a wealth of
sensations; the smooth satiny feel of Ben's skin
and the underlying hard bone; the salt maleness
she could taste beneath her mouth; the heady scent
of it; her need of him so compulsive that she was
barely aware of his curse as he started to jerk away
from her, changing his mind and instead, lowering
his head until his tongue found the sensitive cord
in her neck, his hands pushing aside her towel to
explore and possess the curves beneath.

Outside the storm raged, but it was nothing to
the feelings raging inside her, Sarah thought
weakly as she let Ben lay her on the bed, her hands
going eagerly to his body when he joined her,
pushing the robe off his shoulders, her pulses
thudding when he shrugged it off completely.

A pulse beat tensely against his jaw and she
reached upwards, kissing the spot, feeling his
hands tighten on her body, her lips moving slowly
over his throat, feeling the clenched tension of his
skin as he swallowed, muttering something she
couldn't decipher, before grasping her shoulders,
her protest muffled beneath the hot possession of
his mouth as it took hers in a kiss that had none of
the sophistication she remembered from earlier
kisses, but echoed the savage demand she could
feel exploding inside her and went on until they
were both out of breath, their hearts thudding in

heavy unison, until Ben raised his head and looked at her, his thumb probing the full softness of her lip where she had bitten it earlier.

'Did I do that?'

The look in his eyes made her shake with need. She shook her head, in denial. 'No, it was . . .'

'Don't say it, Sarah,' he warned her, his voice suddenly bitter. 'God, you must have been desperate! Does Dale know the effect storms have on you? A potent stimulant, obviously. Was it he who taught you so well, Sarah? For a moment there you almost had me going out of my mind! But then that was the idea, wasn't it? Just like old times,' he added sardonically. 'Well, if that's the way you want it . . .' Before she could utter a word he bent his head, his tongue teasing the outline of her lips, but Sarah could sense the difference. Whatever it was that had burned between them before was gone. She felt sick and miserable, disgusted by her own lack of will power, hating the coldly assessing way Ben's eyes slid over her body, his hand cupping her breast.

'No!' She pulled sharply away from him, reaching for her towel and pulling it protectively around her.

'Ben, why are you doing this?' she demanded huskily. Why was he tormenting her?

'You really need to ask?' His eyes were cruel. 'You're a very desirable woman, Sarah, and I still want you. You know that, and knowing it, it's up to you to tell me "no". If you don't, you can be sure that sooner or later I'm going to think you're saying "yes", and I don't think Dale's going to like that. You surprise me, you know,' he added, as he stretched out a lazy hand for his robe, totally unconcerned about his nudity. 'I know Dale likes to play the field, but I always thought of you as the type of woman who wants her man all to herself. You and Dale didn't stay together long after you left me, and yet here you are, back in his arms . . .'

A denial trembled on her lips and was instantly silenced. His admission that he wanted her had stunned her and she knew that she wasn't strong enough to resist him if made love to her. Believing that Dale was still her lover might keep him at bay. It would also salve her pride, and so she kept silent.

CHAPTER SIX

'No, Gina, you must look more cowed. Remember Richard is your *beau idéal*, and now you're married to him. And yet you don't know him; you're inclined to be in awe of him.' Ben shouted the directions from where he was standing several feet away from the small group standing by the city walls.

They were filming the execution of the garrison of Acre. Sarah was standing next to Gina, wondering tiredly how many more times they would have to go through the scene. In point of fact the female parts in this scene were very small. All that was required of the three of them, herself as Joanna, Gina Frey as Berengaria, Richard's bride, and Eva as his mother Eleanor, was for them to look on with emotions which would mirror their differing personalities. However, Gina had other ideas, and Sarah could see that Ben was fast losing patience with her. The other woman was miscast, and she was making not the slightest effort to *be* Berengaria, as far as Sarah could see.

'Gina!' Ben was on the point of losing his temper; even Gina looked slightly apprehensive. 'Either you play Berengaria, or you leave this cast,' he grated at her. 'And don't threaten me with R.J. If this goes on much longer, you'll have cost him more money than the rest of the cast put together—and so I shall tell him!'

This time when they went through the scene

Gina was perfect; her distress when the camera homed in on her face, after having witnessed the savagery of her husband's command, sufficiently eloquent for Ben to call tiredly, 'That's it—can it.'

'You'd think she'd realise by now that Ben simply isn't interested in her,' Eva murmured to Sarah as they both went to sit in the shade. The storm had passed leaving the air clearer, but it was still hot, and Sarah wasn't going to be foolish enough to get heatstroke again. Not after what had happened last time! How close she had come to betraying her feelings to Ben!

'I think she took fright when Ben told her he'd get rid of her,' Sarah agreed. She felt hot and tired, her body aching with the effort of standing still for so many takes; funny how standing still was more exhausting than moving about.

'Umm—well, of course he's got a tremendous amount tied up in this film, so it's no wonder he wants it all to be exactly right.'

'As director he does have a lot of responsibility,' Sarah assented.

'Oh, but ...' Eva looked at her, then changed her mind. Sarah didn't press her to continue, but she couldn't help wondering what she had been about to say. Could Ben have money tied up in the film? It wouldn't be totally unusual. He was coming towards them, and despite the gruelling heat and the problems of the morning he looked enviably cool and in control. He flopped down beside them, idly picking up Sarah's hand and holding it loosely between his own. For effect? She longed to pull away, but Eva was talking and would surely have noticed.

'It's coming along very well, Ben,' she said warmly. 'Don't you think so?'

'Umm, we're not doing too badly.' He was noncommittal, his mind obviously on other things, and when Eva excused herself saying that she felt her make-up was in need of attention Sarah wondered if she had left them alone deliberately. Although the crew and cast were all friendly, Sarah often found herself isolated with Ben, almost as though they *were* lovers ... Her face burned at the implication of her thoughts. 'Not getting too hot again, are you?' Ben queried sharply, adding, 'Stay there, I've got something for you.' He disappeared and returned ten minutes or so later, walking from the direction of the vehicles they had used to get the equipment and themselves out to the castle. 'Here.' He tossed a paper package at her, and as she caught it, Sarah frowned. What on earth was it? 'Open it, it won't bite,' he told her lazily, dropping down beside her again. 'I got it yesterday, I had to go to Seville.'

'Again?' That was twice in as many days.

'It's the nearest place I can telephone the States from. Aren't you going to open it?'

She did so reluctantly, amazement mirrored in her eyes as she pulled away the paper to reveal a pretty soft green straw hat, with a brim large enough to shade her face. 'Just see that you wear it,' was Ben's only comment as he watched her try it on, his eyes on Dale, who was lounging by the side of the canteen, ripping the metal tag off a canned drink. Sarah, following the direction of his gaze, frowned. Dale was behaving rather oddly towards her; effusively affectionate one moment

Harlequin Presents...

VIOLET WINSPEAR
time of the temptress

SALLY WENTWORTH
say hello to yesterday

GET
4 BOOKS
FREE

CHARLOTTE LAMB
man's world

ANNE MATHER
born out of love

Say Hello to Yesterday
Holly Weston had done it all alone.

She had raised her small son and worked her way up to features writer for a major newspaper. Still the bitterness of the past seven years lingered.

She had been very young when she married Nick Falconer—but old enough to lose her heart completely when he left. Despite her success in her new life, her old one haunted her.

But it was over and done with—until an assignment in Greece brought her face to face with Nick, and all she was trying to forget. . . .

Time of the Temptress
The game must be played his way!

Rebellion against a cushioned, controlled life had landed Eve Tarrant in Africa. Now only the tough mercenary Wade O'Mara stood between her and possible death in the wild, revolution-torn jungle.

But the real danger was Wade himself—he had made Eve aware of herself as a woman.

"I saved your neck, so you feel you owe me something," Wade said. "But you don't owe me a thing, Eve. Get away from me." She knew she could make him lose his head if she tried. But that wouldn't solve anything. . . .

Your Romantic Adventure Starts Here.

Born Out of Love
It had to be coincidence!

Charlotte stared at the man through a mist of confusion. It was Logan. An older Logan, of course, but unmistakably the man who had ravaged her emotions and then abandoned her all those years ago.

She ought to feel angry. She ought to feel resentful and cheated. Instead, she was apprehensive—terrified at the complications he could create.

"We are not through, Charlotte," he told her flatly. "I sometimes think we haven't even begun."

Man's World
Kate was finished with love for good.

Kate's new boss, features editor Eliot Holman, might have devastating charms—but Kate couldn't care less, even if it was obvious that he was interested in her.

Everyone, including Eliot, though Kate was grieving over the loss of her husband, Toby. She kept it a carefully guarded secret just how cruelly Toby had treated her and how terrified she was of trusting men again.

But Eliot refused to leave her alone, which only served to infuriate her. He was no different from any other man. . . or was he?

and then critically resentful the next. She couldn't blame him for being a little annoyed with her— after all, she had deceived him about her divorce, but the deception hadn't been deliberate, and she missed the companionship they had previously shared. Only this morning he had made a lunge towards her, grabbing her and kissing her, ignoring her breathless protest and causing Ben to frown at them. He had released her with exaggerated care too, Sarah remembered, making some comment about forgetting that she was now 'Ben's property'.

'You might try having a word with Dale about his drinking,' Ben's voice broke in upon her thoughts. 'He's going a bit over the top.'

'I expect he's worried about his part.' Sarah was quick to defend him. 'It can't be easy for him, playing Richard, it's a very demanding role.'

'You think it would have been better to take the easy way out and make some sort of hero out of a legend?' Ben taunted. 'Do you find the script's portrayal of him . . . unacceptable?'

'Because of his lover, do you mean?' Sarah responded frankly. 'No, I don't, but it's typical of you that you should think I might do, Ben. If you want my honest opinion, I think the script deserves half a dozen Oscars. I'd love to meet the writer. I can't remember when I last read anything that showed such a depth of compassion and comprehension. Logically the most one ought to be able to feel for Richard is perhaps pity, but instead when I read the script I found myself actually wishing there was some way there could be a happy ending.'

'With Berengaria?' Ben mocked, his mouth twisting.

'No.' Sarah shook her head. 'With Philip,' she corrected him firmly. 'That's how powerfully the script is written.'

'Because it makes the unacceptable acceptable?' Ben mocked, but he was watching her closely, and Sarah was angry enough to say flatly:

'No, because it shows him as a human being, with virtues and failings, just like any other, and because it has the compassion not to condemn him for them, and I wouldn't like to think myself any less capable of compassion than the man who wrote it—but then I don't suppose that's something you'd be able to understand, Ben,' she said bitterly. 'Compassion doesn't have any place in your life, does it?' Without another word she got up and walked away from him, but even though she had not intended to do so, something made her pause and turn round. He was watching her, and the sunlight dancing on the ground must have played tricks on her eyes because, for a second, he looked almost bereft.

Having lost time at the beginning of the filming, Ben seemed determined to make up for it. He had a gift for directing that enabled him to get the best out of his cast, Sarah was forced to acknowledge, watching him work, one day, waiting for her cue to join some of the male actors, Richard's knights, who were supposedly enjoying an afternoon's hawking.

They were filming her journey through France en route for Spain and her first husband, and shortly she would be joining the others on set, having left her women to hawk with the men. Beneath her the pretty mare she was riding pivoted and tossed her head, and Sarah smoothed her neck automatically, hoping that she would be able to play the scene to Ben's satisfaction. As the rebellious, turbulent teenage Joanna, very much attracted to one of Richard's knights, she had disobeyed her brother's orders that she was to remain with her women and had followed the men on her horse. The script called for her to gallop madly towards Alain de Courcy, losing her veil and the snood constraining her hair as she did so, arriving at his side, flushed and breathless, her hair all in disarray, eagerly showing her feelings for him in her expression, while Paul Howell, the actor playing Alain, had to grasp her bridle in concern and then lean towards her and kiss her.

Her eyes on the group of riders, Sarah watched as Paul detached himself from the others and bent to examine his horse's hoof. This was her cue, and the small mare responded immediately to her touch. She had always enjoyed riding, having learned as a schoolgirl, and it was undeniably pleasant to feel the coolness of a breeze against her face. Blotting out everything but the fact that she *was* Joanna Plantagenet, Sarah disposed of her veil, checking an inward sigh of relief as the snood obediently came away with it, her hair whipping against her face, her eyes lighting up as she saw Alain riding grimly towards her.

'My lady, forgive me, that was not well done of me, I . . .'

'There is no need to apologise, Sir Knight,'

Sarah responded, her lines coming unbidden, hurt rejection glimmering in her eyes as she concentrated on the emotions Joanna would have experienced at being rejected by the man she loved, after their first kiss.

They played the scene to the end without hitch, or interruption from Ben, who only came striding towards them when it was over.

'Ben, I'm not sure about that bit where I kiss her,' Paul commented worriedly. 'My horse moved. Do you want to shoot it again?'

'No.' His voice was terse, his mouth curtly uncompromising as he bit out the word. Paul looked slightly puzzled, but didn't say anything, and Sarah stifled her own surprise. She had been sure that Ben would want them to do the scene again. He had made Dale run through a scene three times the previous day, for an equally small flaw, but perhaps he was worrying about costs, she reflected, as she dismounted and handed the reins of her horse over to the waiting boy. After all, Dale's part was the major role, and yet Ben had been so particular about every aspect of the film. She was still looking puzzled when she saw Eva coming towards her, proffering a cold drink. Ben had gone to talk to the technicians, and Eva asked sympathetically:

'Something wrong?'

'Not really, I was just wondering why Ben didn't want us to re-do that scene.'

'Perhaps he just doesn't like seeing his wife in the arms of another man,' Eva offered with a smile. 'He *is* human, you know,' she added gently, 'and you have only recently been reconciled. I know externally he always seems a cool customer, but we both know that's just a veneer. Dale's the shallow one of the two, for all his much vaunted male macho image.'

There was talk of a party on the final night before they flew to America for the studio filming, which was to include her own love scene, and those scenes which took place before Richard's departure for the Crusade. Sarah wasn't particularly keen to go. There was a limit to how long she could keep up the role of dutiful wife. Although Ben had made no further attempt to touch her and she had been careful to make sure she gave him no excuse for doing so, his words still burned in her mind. She knew she couldn't allow him to make love to her without betraying her real feelings, and anyway, she didn't want only his physical desire. Most nights she heard him typing long after she had gone to bed. She had no idea what he was doing and guessed that he would not tell her even if she were to ask.

She refused the invitation to the party and then discovered that Ben had business in Seville and would not be back until late anyway. He made no suggestion that she accompany him, and although Dale tried to coax her to change her mind, she refused. Trying to be Joanna had taken more out of her than she had anticipated, and combined with the strain of living side by side with Ben, and yet trying to appear indifferent to him, was beginning to tell.

'Oh, come on, sweetling,' Dale protested when she refused. They were standing by his trailer, and he opened the door. 'Come inside and we'll have a drink and talk it over. I'm sure I can persuade you to change your mind.' He gave her a winning smile, but Sarah still shook her head.

'Really I'd rather not, Dale,' she told him firmly. 'I'm whacked.'

'Poor darling!' His voice was caressing and she couldn't avoid the arm he slid round her or the light pressure of his lips as they brushed hers. More exasperated than annoyed, she pushed him away, startled to discover Ben standing less than three yards away, watching them.

'Oh dear,' Dale drawled, 'all is discovered!'

It should have been funny, and she was sure Dale had meant it to be, but somehow it wasn't. Ben looked more contemptuous than amused, and Sarah found to her dismay that she felt sick and shaky, anxiety clawing at her stomach. Without uttering a word, Ben walked away, leaving Dale to pull a far from repentant face. 'He's only being dog-in-the-manger,' he told Sarah easily. 'We both know that. Unless, of course, I was right, and he's made good his old bet? Ben's the type who would believe better late than never, and like I told you, sweetling, he'd do it, just to give himself the pleasure of thinking he'd come between us.'

Her stomach churning unpleasantly, Sarah shook her head. 'You're wrong, Dale,' she announced with more firmness than she felt. 'I know you warned me to be on my guard before, but Ben doesn't ... hasn't ...' She struggled for words, and Dale relaxed.

'That's okay, then,' he said softly. 'I don't want him hurting my favourite girl—not a second time!'

Sarah could still hear the noise of the party when she prepared for bed. On the pretext of needing to read through her lines again she had stayed up until gone twelve, hoping that Ben might return, but he still wasn't back, and even if he had been she didn't quite know what she had hoped for.

At first when she heard the urgent knocking on the trailer door, she thought it was Ben, but when she opened it, it was Paul who stood there, his face creased in anxious concern.

'Sarah, can I have a word with Ben?'

'He isn't here,' she told him slowly. 'He's still in Seville. Can I help?'

'I don't know. It's Dale. He insisted on going into town after the party had finished. I went with him—he wasn't fit to drive, although he threatened that he would, and now . . .'

'He's drunk?' Sarah ventured.

'And how! He's still in the car, and I thought Ben might be able to . . .'

'If you can bring the car up here and we can get him into the trailer, I might be able to get some black coffee into him,' Sarah suggested, 'and then between us we could get him back to his own trailer to sleep it off.'

'Would you?' Paul looked relieved. 'I'll go and get him.'

By the time she heard the car Sarah had the coffee ready. It took the two of them to get Dale into the trailer, and once in he dropped senselessly on to the bunk-like settee, at first refusing all their efforts to get him to drink the coffee.

'We're never going to sober him up. I shouldn't

have involved you in this,' Paul muttered grimly. 'And what makes it worse is that I'm sure he's only doing it to spite Ben. Ben told him to cool his drinking and this is his way of getting back at him. He knows quite well the film's gone too far now for Ben to replace him, and if he starts delaying things now, making Ben waste time while he gets him sobered up, the backers are going to come down hard on Ben.'

He made it sound almost as though Dale hated Ben, Sarah thought. And she was just turning this thought over in her mind, when Paul gave a cry of pain as Dale moved, jerkily, and the mug of boiling hot coffee tipped over his wrist and hand, soaking through his jeans.

'You go and get changed,' Sarah told him as she mopped up the mess. 'Dale seems to be coming out of it now. I'll try and get some coffee into him while you're gone.'

'Thanks. I'll be as quick as I can.'

'Come on, Dale, drink this.' Paul had been gone for just over ten minutes, and Dale mumbled something unintelligible as Sarah held the mug to his mouth. At least he was sitting upright now, she thought tiredly. With any luck, by the time Paul returned, Dale would be able to make it to his own trailer under his own steam.

'Don't look at me like that, sweetling,' Dale remonstrated in slurred tones. 'Just because I had a good time! You're getting almost as bad as that husband of yours. Where is he, by the way?' he asked, looking round the trailer. 'Not gone off and left you, has he? Poor Sarah, we'll have to do something about that, won't we?'

'Dale, stop it!' Sarah protested as he put his arm round her, leaning drunkenly against her, his lips moving along her jaw. For someone who was drunk he showed surprising strength and determination, and Sarah grasped him crossly, trying to push him away. He didn't realise what he was doing, of course. He couldn't.

'Lovely Sarah,' he muttered thickly as she tried to move him, pressing his mouth against her throat. If she couldn't move him then she would have to move herself, Sarah decided despairingly, not realising as she pulled away that he was half lying on her robe. There was a brief tearing sound as she moved, but the words of protest she was about to utter were lost as the trailer door suddenly opened and she saw Ben looking down at them.

The look on his face beggared words, and Sarah felt herself flushing crimson with guilt as she realised that he had completely misinterpreted the scene.

'Couldn't he even wait to get you to bed?' Ben snarled at last. Adding grimly, 'I warned you, Sarah!'

'But Ben . . .' He's drunk, she had been about to say, but Dale suddenly lifted his head and looked at them, the smile he gave Ben bringing a dark tide of anger to the latter's face. Sarah shrank back as Ben reached for Dale, half dragging and half lifting him out of his seat.

'Ben, please, you don't understand,' Sarah protested, reading murder in the hot fury of his eyes.

'Be quiet!' he gritted at her. 'I'll deal with you

later.' Almost throwing Dale out of the trailer, he
turned and followed him, while Sarah held her
breath, praying that Paul would return in time for
them to explain.

'I know you're burning to thump me, Ben,' she
heard Dale say, suddenly far more sober than he
had been in the trailer, 'but if you break my jaw,
you'll only delay completion of the film. Never
mind,' he mocked, and Sarah shivered at his
foolhardiness,'third time lucky!'

How could he remind Ben of the first time he
had found them together in compromising circum-
stances? The look on her husband's face had
shown all too clearly that his anger had exploded
out of control, and Sarah was shivering when she
heard him return.

'Dale might have got off scot-free,' she heard
him saying suavely somewhere above her as he
closed the door, 'but you're not going to! I'll have
to think of a punishment that won't show; won't
spoil that pale skin and delay filming, won't I, my
dear wife?' He almost snarled the last words, and
Sarah shrank from him as he reached down and
with one violent movement ripped both what was
left of her robe and the fine lawn nightgown she
was wearing beneath it.

'Ben, please!' she begged in a last-ditch attempt to
deflect the violence of his rage, but it wasn't any use,
his hands were already on her body, and Sarah
shivered as he swung her up into his arms and
carried her the few yards to his bedroom. In contrast
to the untidiness of the area where he worked in the
trailer, everything was immaculately neat, the bed
made and the room somehow impersonal. She

wasn't going to fight against him, she decided resignedly; she would only lose, and anyway she had a sickening suspicion that that was exactly what he wanted her to do, and that the demons that rode him would enjoy punishing her folly if she did, but a deep-seated feminine instinct that wouldn't be denied made her cringe instinctively from him when he dropped her callously on the bed and then turned to take off his clothes, his eyes glittering savagely as he subjected her pale body to a slow and insulting inspection that left her flushed and humiliated, wishing she could match him look for look. But somehow her glance skidded uncertainly from broad male shoulders, downwards to the hard flatness of his belly, registering somewhere along the way that his tan extended to every inch of his body, and wondering with a swift stab of jealousy if he sunbathed alone, or if someone had been with him, and if so, if he had turned to her in the drowsy heat of a Californian afternoon, and they had made love.

'Frightened?' He purred the word with all the deceptive softness of a jungle cat before demolishing its prey. 'No need to be, I'm only taking what's rightfully mine.'

'There's now a law that forbids a man to rape his wife—just in case you didn't know,' Sarah warned him, wishing her voice didn't sound quite so breathless, but her words seemed to have no effect upon him at all, he simply walked round the bed still watching her, studying her, and she had to fight against her need to protect herself from the narrowed and mocking assessment of his gaze by reaching for some form of cover.

'Shy?' The mocking jibe stung, and she gasped a

protest as Ben suddenly sat down beside her, reaching for her hands, and uncurling the fingers she hadn't realised were digging into the softness of the duvet. 'There's really no need to be,' Ben drawled softly. 'After all, the entire film-going world has seen you like this at one time or another, if only briefly.'

There had been a scene similar to this in *Shakespeare*, Sarah remembered, and how she had hated filming it, but it had been very brief and she hadn't been completely nude, and then Ben had been tender and understanding, helping her through what was for her a formidable ordeal. 'And Dale, of course,' Ben added, not quite as softly, moving slightly so that he was lying beside her, his head supported by his hand as he continued to study her. In spite of her fear, Sarah felt an immediate response. Her mind was a frantic ball of fear, tensed inside her skull, but her body ... 'But tonight you're going to forget him.'

'Don't say a word,' he warned her, when she opened her mouth to protest, and then his mouth was hard and angry on hers, deliberately punishing and inflicting hurt. She struggled against him, but his hands slid from her shoulders to her waist, digging into the vulnerable flesh.

Her struggles brought her into closer contact with his body, her breasts pressed against his chest, the friction of his hair-roughened flesh against their sensitive tips instantly arousing. Anger and despair burned through her, mingling with her love and need; she hated him for what he was trying to do to her; for all that he had already done to her, and yet she still loved him; yearned for him to love her with a matching intensity.

When Ben released her mouth it was throbbing from the violence of his kiss, his eyes brilliantly green as he looked down into her face. 'What's the matter?' he mocked. 'Too scared to fight?'

Something seemed to explode inside her, and her body tensed under the force of the emotion burning through her, her hand lifting to claw at the arrogantly mocking face.

Just for a moment she thought she glimpsed satisfaction in Ben's eyes as his fingers closed on her wrist, forcing her arm down to her side, his mouth on hers demanding a bitter tribute from the vanquished to the victor. A red mist seemed to dance before her eyes, a savage, choking feeling racing through her veins, her body tensing against the hard presence of Ben's hand cupping her breast, the hand he had released forming a small fist to hammer unavailingly at the breadth of his shoulders, while all the time the molten anger kept on growing and changing, so gradually that she didn't realise that anger had given way to an equally fierce passion, her body responding to Ben's with an intensity which surely betrayed her in a hundred ways. But when she looked into his face, there was no recognition of his victory there, the normally acutely perceptive green eyes hazed by a desire which she recognised was as strong as her own.

'Sarah.' He muttered her name thickly, as though he was barely aware of having done so, his hand tangling in her hair, tugging back her head, exposing the vulnerable column of her throat.

When his mouth moved over it she thought she would die of the explosive pleasure shooting through her body, and realised with passion-distorted haziness that he was as much in the grip of desire as she was herself; rationality suspended as their bodies took over from their minds. A tiny detached corner of hers registered that he was breathing harshly, his forehead damp as it rested against her skin, a dark flush colouring his skin, his hands trembling faintly against her body as his mouth burned compulsively against her skin, the savage teeth of anger softened by their mutual passion.

When his mouth left her throat she was shivering, shaking with something she no longer wanted to pretend was fear, the pressure of her fingers digging into the hardness of his back indicative not of anger, but of need, an inner instinct telling her that no matter what had motivated Ben originally, it, and his habitual cool control, were both suspended. Dimly she realised how much she had yearned to see him like this, as much a victim of need as she was herself, something she had always thought missing when he made love to her in the past. Even when he had finally possessed her she had been conscious of a holding back; a fine control.

'Sarah, touch me. Want me!' The words shivered across her skin, muttered against it, his gaze burning feverishly into her as he looked the length of her body, his eyes darkening in acknowledged arousal as his hands cupped her breasts witnessing the evidence of how he had affected her, her body unashamedly arching invitingly as he lowered his head and touched first one and then the other swollen nipple with his lips and then again with his tongue. Desire ran like quicksilver from the heat of his mouth on her body to every nerve ending, her nails biting deep in mute ecstasy against his skin. Through the melting pleasure his touch was giving her Sarah felt him tense, mutter something against her skin, and then possess the swollen fullness of one breast, sucking it with a compulsive hunger, which she knew once would have shocked her, but now only awoke a corresponding hunger within her to touch him, driving her to press her body closer to his in an aching frenzy of need, her hands moving hungrily over the satin smoothness of his skin, exploring the male shape of him as she had never done before, marvelling at the variety of sensations relayed to her as her fingertips moved over his body, and finding a deeply intense pleasure in Ben's shuddering response to her exploration; his hoarsely muttered insistence that she touch him with her mouth as well as with her hands, and her own eagerness to comply.

The climax was as frenetic as all that had gone before, Sarah aching for the complete fulfilment of Ben's possession long minutes before it was accomplished, when she sensed he denied them both to intensify their eventual mutual pleasure. But his control was obviously greater than hers, her need only briefly appeased by the hard urgency of his body against hers, whispered pleas mingled with the kisses she pressed against his skin, her tongue delighting in the faintly salt taste of him as it moved along his throat, her body registering the

tense response of his muscles to her touch with a
shivering delight that when communicated to him
dissolved the last barrier of his control, his hands
and mouth suddenly urgent in their demands, her
cries of pleasure lost beneath his kiss, both of them
abandoning themselves to the shuddering crescendo of pleasure.

Afterwards, lying limp and exhausted in his
arms, Sarah could barely comprehend what had
happened; how punishment had turned to pleasure,
anger igniting a passion which had burned with
unanticipated ferocity. She glanced at Ben. He was
lying with his eyes closed, but they opened as
though he sensed her look. Quite what she had
expected him to say, she wasn't sure, but when he
turned to her and said perfectly evenly and
mockingly, '*Now* tell me about Dale,' the fragile
illusion that they had shared something rare and
precious shattered into a thousand irreparable
fragments. Half a dozen retorts sprang to her lips,
only to be discarded. He had tricked her again.
What she had thought of as shared passion had
obviously all been a sham. In a daze of pain she
heard him adding insultingly, 'I'll say one thing for
him, though, he's taught you to be a woman,
Sarah, and a very passionate one. Perhaps it's a
pity after all that you don't have any major love
scene in *Richard*. You're wasting a very excellent
talent, my dear. You could make a fortune from
appearing in . . .'

She hit him before he could continue, the
imprint of her hand leaving a white and then red
mark against his face. Tears threatened, and
without waiting to see his reaction she fled,

terrified with every thudding heartbeat that he would pursue. Only when she had been lying in her own bed for half an hour did she realise that he wouldn't, and only then did she acknowledge that her punishment was perhaps that he had not.

What they had shared in making love had opened her eyes to many things she had not previously known; among them her own deeply passionate nature. Ben had made love to her to punish her, but even knowing that she hadn't been able to stop herself responding. Thank God they were leaving Spain in the morning, she thought achingly. She could not endure to live in such close confines with Ben any longer. He must surely have guessed how she felt about him. He hadn't taunted her with it yet, but no doubt he would. And it wasn't until she was on the point of sleep that she remembered Dale, and the original cause of Ben's anger.

'Well, that's that,' Lois exclaimed. 'Everything packed up and ready to go. I must admit I'm looking forward to getting back. My boy-friend works for a local radio station,' she explained, 'and being away on location without him is hell!'

Sarah had gone to see her to find out what arrangements had been made for her journey to Hollywood. She had learned that seats had been booked on flights for all the cast and crew. 'Although of course Gina is returning with R.J., in his private plane.' She pulled a face and grimaced. 'Poor guy, he's quite sweet, I don't think he honestly deserves her—she's such a bitch.'

R.J. had arrived the previous evening, just in

time to join the party, but because Sarah hadn't gone she hadn't seen him until the morning when he had arrived to discuss the film with Ben.

Sarah had been making coffee when Ben brought him in, and after being introduced, she had made herself scarce, realising that they wanted to talk privately. In fact she was only too glad not to have to face Ben alone. She had woken hating herself for what had happened between them, not knowing how on earth she was going to endure the mocking comments she was sure must be on the edge of his tongue.

'Sarah!'

She flushed wildly and turned, hearing Ben's voice, relieved to find that R.J. was still with him.

'R.J.'s offered us both a ride back in his private jet, and I've accepted. It will give you a few hours to get settled into the house before we get on with the rest of the filming.'

'The house?' Sarah eyed him uncertainly, and was rewarded with a briefly impatient frown.

'Yes, my house, on Malibu beach. I prefer to live there, and it isn't too far to the studio, or the location where we'll do the rest of the filming.'

'But . . .' but I don't want to stay with you, had been the words trembling on her lips, but she sensed that to utter them would bring down fresh censure on her head, and she felt too tired and drained to argue. Of course Ben would want this fiction of a marriage to continue until after he had completed work on the film. But how long would that be? How much longer could she endure? At least one small blessing was that in a house there would be more opportunity to avoid one another.

Last night, for instance, she had lain sleepless listening to the sound of him breathing, knowing that only a thin wall separated them. A thin wall ... and a wide gulf embattled with contempt and deceit on Ben's side, and disillusionment and despair on hers, she decided tiredly.

CHAPTER SEVEN

How bare everything looked with the equipment half dismantled, Sarah thought, studying the activity going on all around her. Later, when they had all gone, the hire company would come to remove the trailers and then there would be nothing left to even show that they had been there; at least not outwardly. Rather like her relationship with Ben, she thought tiredly. Outwardly it might never have happened, but inwardly ... She stiffened slightly as she saw the object of her thoughts approaching, her muscles as tense as an angry cat's, ready to scratch rather than purr.

'I thought you finished packing half an hour ago,' was his opening comment, but Sarah didn't miss the way his eyes hardened over her closed and withdrawn expression, or the tautly controlled anger which seemed to emanate from him as he stood watching her, his body tautly lean, the action of sliding his hands into the pockets of his jeans drawing attention to the powerful strength of his thighs and their wholly male structure. Deeply flushed, she looked away, trying to control breathing suddenly as laboured as though she had been running.

'Sarah!' Her head snapped up as she heard someone call her name. Paul came loping towards her, his dark hair damp, a bronze sheen on his deeply tanned skin. By anyone else's standards he

116

was undoubtedly a very handsome man, Sarah acknowledged, forcing a smile, but he didn't possess one tenth of the sensual magnetism of the man standing next to her.

'I just wanted to thank you for helping out last night,' Paul began as he drew level with them. 'I did start to come back when I'd dealt with my arm, but when I got to Dale's trailer I saw he was in it, and comparatively sober as well.' He turned to Ben and grimaced. 'He gave us both a hard time, Ben, and Sarah was a real good Samaritan, offering to help me with him when I came to the trailer looking for you.' With another smile he sauntered off, leaving Sarah alone with Ben in a silence that seemed fraught with unspoken undercurrents.

'What was all that about?' Ben's voice was perfectly even, but nevertheless Sarah shivered as much as if the temperature had suddenly dropped by ten degrees.

'Sarah!' His tone warned her that he was getting impatient. 'Tell me,' he demanded.

'You heard Paul,' she returned, trying to match his cool dryness of tone. 'He knocked on the trailer door some time after twelve last night. At first I thought it was you. He explained that Dale had ... had been into town,' she hesitated a little over the words, not wanting to betray to him Dale's recklessness, but realised her small subterfuge had been in vain when Ben's mouth twisted and he said sardonically:

'Had got himself so drunk that Paul had to bring him back half insensible, is that what you mean?'

'He . . . he had been drinking,' Sarah agreed, trying to avoid the question. 'Paul wanted to try and . . . sober him up. He'd come to you for help, and I . . .'

'And you naturally leapt into the breach,' Ben sneered. 'But that still doesn't explain how I came to find you in his arms, does it? Or do you want him so much that you don't mind being mauled by someone in his condition?'

'It wasn't like that!'

'No? Then tell me what it was like?' Suddenly he seemed to have moved much too close to her, his fingers curling round her arm, and Sarah had the impression that if he could he'd like to shake the truth out of her.

'I made him some coffee, but as we were trying to get him to drink it, it spilled over Paul and he had to go and change and see to his arm. When he had gone, Dale . . .'

'I think I can guess for myself what Dale did when he was alone with you,' Ben interrupted, his voice suddenly as dangerous as broken glass. 'Did it never occur to you that for a man in his supposed state he sobered up quickly enough when I appeared?'

It *had* struck her that Dale had made a remarkably swift recovery, and although she wasn't going to say as much to Ben, her expression gave her away, and he drawled sardonically, 'And taking that a step further, might it just be possible that Dale manoeuvred Paul deliberately, using him to . . .'

'To be alone with me?' Sarah demanded, her temper suddenly rising. Why did everyone try to blacken Dale? 'If Dale wants to be alone with me, he doesn't need to resort to subterfuge.'

'Not unless he wants me to be a witness to it,' Ben agreed, watching the emotions chase one another across her face.

'But why ... why should he want to do that?' Just for a moment Sarah felt as though she teetered on the edge of some breathtaking discovery; something so important and monumental that her mind reeled with the power of it, but no sooner had she grasped the possibility than it eluded her, and Ben's face, grimly closed and hard with anger, mocked the vulnerability of her thoughts.

'Leave it, Sarah,' he advised her grittily. 'You've just overplayed your hand.' He released her and walked away without a backward glance; leaving her smouldering with fresh anger. There hadn't been so much as an apology for last night; for wrongly accusing her, for ... making love to her. Her heart thudded in suddenly accelerated confusion. Had she expected him to apologise? To tell her that he had made love to her out of desire and want, rather than anger? But there *had* been desire, she protested fiercely, and not just on her part.

'Just as soon as we take off I'll have the steward bring you a drink.'

They were in the cabin of R.J.'s private jet, and Sarah was still staring wonderingly around her, marvelling at the luxury of it. Gina was lying back in her own seat, eyes closed, her expression one of bored petulance, rejecting every attempt on the part of her lover to placate her.

Sarah had half expected her to insist on sitting with Ben, but it was evident that much as she wanted Ben, she wasn't prepared to risk losing her rich lover to get him, and Sarah could well imagine how that would gall a man of Ben's temperament. He would never stand for coming second—in any woman's affections.

Their take-off was smooth, the steward moving swiftly to dispense drinks. Sarah asked for something long and cold, and settled back in her seat to drink it. Ben was sitting next to her, and even without looking at him she was conscious of his proximity, wave after wave of heat suffusing her body as she recognised the intensity of her own desire to touch and be touched by him. She jerked her thoughts away from Ben painfully, to hear R.J. saying, 'I've got a little surprise for you, Ben—instead of the traditional film, we're going to watch the rushes. This husband of yours is in a class of his own,' R.J. told Sarah whimsically. 'Unlike every other director I know, he won't watch the rushes daily. He prefers to wait.'

'Because I like to see each piece of film cold,' Ben told him. 'When a scene's been freshly filmed my own reaction to it's still clouded by whatever I felt when it was done. I prefer to see it without the rose-tinted lenses.'

'Darling, you're too fussy,' Gina pouted. 'And so very strict!' She glanced at her lover. 'You wouldn't believe how nasty he's been to me!'

If the words held a suggestion of threat R.J. obviously didn't hear it. Instead, much to Sarah's surprise, he beamed. 'That's what I like to hear,' he told Ben, clapping him on the back, 'someone else being careful with my money.'

'Not just yours, darling,' Gina protested, flashing Ben a distinctly provocative look. 'Ben's invested in the film, too. Some day he's going to be nearly as rich as you.'

Once again the financier didn't rise to the bait, instead calling over the steward and murmuring some instructions. Within seconds the cabin was darkened, the screen seeming to appear like magic from the ceiling, and Sarah found that she was holding her breath as she watched.

'Well, darling, what do you think?' Gina lit a cigarette, as light once again flooded the cabin, leaning back in her seat in a pose Sarah thought was probably deliberately provocative, showing off the lines of her body in her thin silk suit.

'It's taking shape,' was Ben's only response, and yet Sarah had been sure that he was pleased, sensing it more from his silence and stillness as they watched the rushes than from any verbal comment he had made.

Her own scenes she had scrutinised carefully, holding her breath as she watched the one with Paul when he kissed her. The small flaw had been carefully edited out, and she frowned, wondering who had noticed, and how the studio had known to take it out.

Some time during the afternoon the effects of her sleepless night and the long flight overtook her. Through the waves of sleep engulfing her Sarah had a hazy impression of Ben bending over her, and the armrest between them being removed, his arm securing her against the length of his body,

but it was just her imagination, she told herself.
Ben had no desire at all to hold her in his arms.

She woke to a sensation of warmth and
languorous happiness, opening her eyes slowly as
she stretched, suddenly aware that she was
pillowed against Ben's side, her head resting just
below his shoulder, her body turned into his. His
arm was round her, his hand curving possessively
just below the swell of her breast. She moved
slightly and felt the pressure of his arm tighten,
a muttered protest alerting her to the fact that
he was still asleep. On the other side of the cabin
she could see the motionless figure of Gina, and
raised herself slowly, taking care not to disturb
Ben, as she looked down into his sleeping face,
unprotected and vulnerable, its harshness softened by the thick sweep of his dark lashes,
wondering a little at the acute weakening well of
protective love the sight of him stirred within
her. Even the hard lines of his mouth seemed
softer, the full underlip denoting the intensity of
his passion.

He stirred and opened his eyes, still glazed with
sleep, his 'Sarah! Darling!' stirred her senses in
much the same way that his expelled breath stirred
the tendrils of hair at her temples, her defences
unprepared for the warm pressure of his hand as it
slid into her hair, propelling her against him, her
mouth parting instinctively to the slow movement
of his lips against hers, Ben's eyes closing again as
his tongue gently explored the shape of her mouth,
so slowly and seductively that it was like drowning
in honey.

'Hey, come on, you two lovebirds! Time for breakfast!'

R.J.'s voice interrupted them, and Ben's eyes opened and hardened as they took in her flushed cheeks and slightly swollen mouth. 'What a pity Dale can't be the one to interrupt *us* now,' he whispered as he released her. 'Do you think he'd be disillusioned?'

His look and the tone of his voice reminded her of everything that she would rather forget.

'Dale knows I'm an actress, Ben,' she retorted, sounding braver than she felt. 'He knows I can always pretend that the man holding me in his arms is the one I really want.'

'Is that so? Then perhaps I ought to have had a tape beside me the other night.' His voice was ugly now, and she flinched from the acidity of it. 'It was my name you called, Sarah, me who you begged to make love to you? Remember?'

She was thankful that the sudden arrival of the steward meant that she needn't reply. He had come to take their order for breakfast, and she numbly asked him simply for a cup of coffee. shuddering as Ben drawled that he was hungry enough for a full breakfast. Her stomach was churning so much she doubted she could even drink her coffee, but their exchange patently hadn't affected Ben in the slightest. But then when had she ever touched his emotions? If he had cared in the slightest about her he would never have tried to make good his bet!

'Welcome to America.' Ben's tone was sardonic rather than welcoming, and Sarah fought to control the clenching muscles of her stomach as the hot sunshine of the Californian morning hit her. Thanks to R.J. they were whisked through Immigration in next to no time—Sarah had been a little startled to discover that Ben had retained his U.K. citizenship and was forced to go through Immigration with her. His work as a film director surely meant that he would spend the rest of his life in and around Hollywood, and she had never heard him say anything that might prove him to be inordinately proud of being British. But then she knew so little about him, she reflected miserably.

'This way.' A cool touch on her arm directed her to a line of waiting cars, and Ben came to rest beside a sleekly elegant black limousine. The chauffeur greeted him with a smile, glancing curiously at Sarah. 'My wife,' Ben informed him as he opened the door for her, then slid inside the cool welcome of the car.

'Which do you want, Mr de l'Isle,' the chauffeur asked him, 'the studio or your home?'

'Home, please, Ray,' Ben replied easily. 'Sarah will want to get settled in, but you can tell Andy I'll be in this afternoon. Ray drives for the studio, not for me,' Ben explained to Sarah as he settled back beside her. 'I've got a meeting there this afternoon. Try not to miss me too much, although I should be back for dinner.'

The mockery in his glance reminded Sarah, if she was in any need of a reminder, that the comment was for the benefit of their driver rather than for her, and she forced her glance away from the dark power of Ben's features and tried to study the scene outside the car. The highway they were travelling along was far wider than anything she had experienced before, packed with glittering pieces of metal. The ultimate consumer society, she found herself thinking as she studied the billboards and the obvious affluence surrounding her.

'We won't go into Hollywood,' Ben told her. 'Plenty of time for you to see that later. We'll take the coast road, Ray,' he told the driver, 'it should be quieter.'

The beauty of the countryside caught Sarah's breath, the tantalising glimpses she had of the ocean making her long for Ray to stop the car so that she could see more, and then the road was sweeping past luxurious and well-tended houses, dropping closer to the coast until it ran parallel to the beach, giving Sarah her first sight of what Ben told her drawlingly were 'beach houses'. Where on earth had she got the idea that they were simple dwellings constructed out of timber and built mainly on stilts? These houses were magnificent, breath-catching, their views only to be guessed at.

'I'll have to drop you there,' Ray announced suddenly, turning to grin at Ben. 'I daren't risk this along that apology you call a road.'

'Don't worry about it. We can use the Range Rover to go the rest of the way.'

'Do you want me to pick you up later?'

Ben shook his head. 'No need. I'll drive myself in.' He opened his door and slid out as Ray came round to help Sarah. The first thing that struck her was the dazing heat; the second the sudden sensation of disorientation. Ray was helping Ben with the cases, and then suddenly he was backing the car, turning it, and leaving them completely alone on what appeared to be a deserted stretch of road.

'This way,' Ben touched her arm, and Sarah withdrew from his touch as though it stung, barely aware of the grimly sardonic twist to his features. 'What's the matter?' he drawled as he led the way to a concrete building Sarah vaguely realised must be a garage. 'Hoping we'd be close enough to Hollywood for you to see lover-boy pretty regularly?' He shook his head. 'I don't mix with that crowd, Sarah. It's pretty remote down here. In fact this track . . .' he indicated the dust grooves in the tussocky sand, 'leads only to my house, so if it's company you want, you'll have to rely on mine.'

He opened the garage door and disappeared inside. She heard an engine fire and stood well back as a Range Rover appeared. 'Come on, get in.' Ben opened the door and leaned down, half lifting and half pulling her in, before completing his reversing manoeuvre. Before he closed the garage with some electronic device she caught a glimpse of a dark, expensive-looking saloon car, and then he was turning, facing down the narrow rutted track.

'You obviously like isolation.' Her voice sounded dry and cracked, edged with tension and pain.

Ben shrugged. 'I certainly prefer no company to the wrong company.' He turned to study her. 'Unlike you. How many men have there been in your life as well as Dale, Sarah? What sort of relationship is it you have with him, anyway? He isn't exactly the faithful type. What is it? An open affair, each of you free to do your own thing when the other isn't around?'

'There hasn't been anyone,' Sarah retorted hotly, just managing to catch back the words 'apart from you', shuddering to think of the effect of such a damning admission.

'You know, you say that emotively enough for it to be true.' He studied her again. 'But haven't you forgotten something? Or rather should I say "someone",' he added pointedly, and she flushed as she realised he was referring to himself. 'They say a woman never forgets her first lover, and I was the first, wasn't I, Sarah?'

Her voice seemed to have locked in her throat, her vocal chords incapable of uttering a sound. 'I ... I don't want to talk about it,' she managed huskily at last.

'Because you hate yourself so much?' he taunted, but beneath the taunting Sarah sensed a deep seam of anger, tightly held under control, and it frightened her, making her glad when the Range Rover suddenly came to a halt at the entrance to a small bay.

'This beach is strictly private,' Ben told her as he climbed lithely out. She heard him coming alongside her, and panicked, thrusting open her door, half stumbling in her anxiety to get out before he could touch her. Her haste was her undoing, and she felt her feet slip from beneath her, her breath arrested as she heard Ben curse, hard hands grasping her waist, his body cushioning her from the fall as she was pressed along the hard length of it.

For a moment it seemed that time stood still,

her heart thudding painfully against her ribs, her
eyes for once on a level with Ben's, hers wide and
startled, his dark and unfathomable, then he started
to lower her to the ground, still holding her against
his body, his head lowering with her descent, his
arms suddenly clamping bruisingly round her. She
knew long before his mouth touched hers that he
was going to kiss her. Dry-mouthed and shaking,
she could only stare up at him, her voice an
inarticulate murmur as his head blotted out the
sunlight and hot delight burned through her. She felt
light, almost boneless in his arms, closing her mind
to reason and letting her hands slide up and into the
thickness of his hair. His body tensed and then he
was kissing her with hungry insistence, tasting the
warm sweetness of her soft lips, making her open her
mouth to him, her body drenched in such a fierce
thrust of pleasure that she murmured his name
involuntarily against his lips. Instantly she was
thrust away from him, contemptuous eyes raking
her trembling form.

'Tell me again that when I hold you you pretend
I'm Dale?' he murmured tauntingly. 'You might be
able to persuade your heart and mind to reject me,
Sarah, but your body feels differently,' and as
though to emphasise the validity of his claim his
hand moved slowly over her, stroking upwards
over the curve of her hip and the narrowness of
her waist coming to rest against the aching curve
of her breast, his thumb stretching the fine fabric
of her blouse until the betraying arousal of her
nipple was plainly visible through the thin cloth.
With a smile of triumph Ben let her go, returning
to the Range Rover to remove their cases.

Following him round to the back, as they turned a corner, Sarah caught her first glimpse of his house. The land rose sharply, sheltering the small bay, and halfway up it on what appeared to be a plateau was Ben's house. Steps led up to it, and the hillside had been planted with a variety of ground-hugging plants, many of which were in bloom. Two tall cypresses guarded the tall grilled gate at the top of the steps. Sarah was out of breath from climbing them, but Ben, who had their cases, seemed unaffected by the climb. She stood aside as he unlocked the gate, and studied the stone wall which ran in either direction away from it.

'It keeps out unwanted visitors,' Ben drawled, following her glance. 'I like my privacy.'

As she stepped through the gate, Sarah couldn't repress a small gasp of delight. She was in a courtyard-style garden, flagged and sunny, a fountain tinkling melodically somewhere unseen, the corners shadowed with trees, green and restful. In front of her patio doors opened out on to the courtyard, and looking up Sarah saw another flight of steps leading up to what was obviously one of the bedrooms, ending on an attractive balcony. The balcony boasted a table and chairs. 'I like to breakfast there,' Ben told her, glancing upwards, then taking her arm and leading her through another archway into what she supposed must be the garden proper with neatly tended lawns, and roses which sprawled lavishly against the stone walls.

The house itself was long and low, apparently built in an 'E' shape, to take advantage of the lie

of the land and get the maximum views, Ben told
her when she remarked on it, hurrying her along
so that she had barely time to glimpse into the
rooms through the windows they passed. The
middle section of the 'E' was a huge garden room,
and Sarah was still gazing at this when they
rounded the corner and she saw the graceful lines
of the pool and its surrounding patio. Then they
were past it and turning to walk down the side of
the house to what she had thought to be the back
but was, she realised, the front, complete with
curling drive. Puzzled, she stared at it, wondering
why Ben hadn't driven straight up, and humour
touched his mouth as he watched and read her
mind. 'It looks very impressive, but it doesn't go
anywhere,' he explained at last. 'This house was
built for a would-be millionaire who went broke
before it was finished. The minute I saw it I knew
it was exactly what I wanted. Californians are
rather fonder of driving than they are of walking.'

'So you bought it to preserve your solitude?'

As a busy director, Sarah couldn't feel that he
would have much time alone, but she didn't
comment, but followed him into an oval hall from
which a white staircase curved graciously upwards.
The hall floor was tiled in marble, the walls a soft
shimmering green. As she looked she heard
footsteps and a plump Mexican woman appeared,
beaming at Ben, then looking at Sarah.

'Margarita, this is my wife. Sarah, meet
Margarita, my housekeeper. Between them she
and Ramón, her husband, look after my home.'

Margarita grinned. 'Your wife, huh?' she
announced with an American twang. 'Perhaps

there won't be so many nights spent working in your study now, eh?'

Ben shook his head, and murmured something in Spanish to which the other woman replied, laughing and looking sideways at Sarah. 'I'll go and fix you both something to eat,' she told them. 'Ramón is collecting the groceries. He'll attend to the bags when he gets back.'

'What was she laughing about?' Sarah demanded, hot-cheeked, when Margarita had disappeared. She had always been sensitive about being laughed at, especially when she didn't know why.

'The fact that I've told her we'll be having separate rooms. I do tend to work a lot at night, and I told her I didn't want to disturb you.'

'To which she replied?' Sarah demanded, not knowing whether to be glad or disappointed about what he had just said.

'Merely that as my woman you'd rather be disturbed than left to lie in a cold bed. Her words, not mine,' he added with a dismissive shrug. 'I could have told her that you've got your love to keep you warm, but somehow I don't think she'd have understood.'

They ate in silence, in an attractive room overlooking the gardens, Sarah barely able to do more than toy with the delicious cold soup Margarita had served. Ben had showered and changed before coming down to lunch, and his hair was still damp, his body tautly muscular in the thin lightweight grey suit he was wearing. To eat he had discarded his jacket and the silk of his shirt clung lovingly to his body, her awareness of him so intense that she was oblivious to everything else. It took a real effort of will to drag her eyes away from him and concentrate on her meal, and she didn't realise how tense she had become until Ben pushed back his chair, the scraping sound rasping along her raw nerves.

'I'm going to the studio. You look tired,' he added curtly. 'Try and have a sleep—you're filming in the morning.'

'When will you be back?' Her voice was stilted and she bit her lip, vexed at her folly, when he raised an eyebrow, his eyes glinting mockingly.

'How very wifely you sound! I'll have to respond in like manner, won't I?' And then he was bending over her, her nostrils suddenly full of the arousing scents of his body, his damp hair brushing against her cheek as his fingers captured her jaw and his mouth touched hers, lightly tormenting, making her long to reach up and hold his mouth against her, her body aching for him to want her. 'In answer to your question,' he murmured when he released her lips, 'I don't know, but don't wait dinner—and don't wait up, unless of course you're prepared to take the consequences.'

He was gone before Sarah could speak, leaving her bemused and shaken. What had his last words meant? That he still wanted her? If she did wait up for him would he take her in his arms and carry her up that curving flight of stairs, and then make love to her as her feverish body ached for him to make love? But for how long would a purely physical act satisfy her starving senses? Oh, initially perhaps it would suffice, but later, when her heart ached to hear words of love; when her soul cried out for more communication than that offered by his body, how would she feel then?

In the end there was no decision to make. She went upstairs, intending merely to lie down for half an hour, but it was dark when she eventually awoke from a deep sleep to discover that someone had thrown a cover over her naked body and that the clock beside her bed showed just gone two.

Beside her was the towel in which she had wrapped herself after her shower. She remembered walking into her room and sitting down on the bed, intending to dry her hair. She must have fallen asleep then. No doubt Margarita had found her when she came to ask what she wanted for dinner. Had Ben returned? The house was in silence. Or was it? Sarah frowned and slid out of bed, opening her door, her ears straining for the familiar sound, her face relaxing when she heard it. Somewhere Ben was typing; she recognised the rattling staccato sound. What on earth was he working on so late into the night? Reminding herself that he was hardly likely to tell her, she set the alarm and climbed back into bed.

When the alarm went off at four she was glad of her extra hours of sleep. Showering quickly, drying herself and putting on fresh underwear, she set to work on her hair, the hair-dryer drowning out the click of her bedroom door, her first intimation that she wasn't alone coming when she glanced in the mirror and saw Ben standing behind her, carrying a tray.

'Breakfast,' he told her, putting it down on a small table. 'Sleep all right?'

She didn't know why, but the look on his face made her colour deeply, wishing she was wearing more than just her brief silk bra and matching French knickers.

'Very well,' she assured him, fighting for composure. He had stopped looking at her face and his eyes had dropped to her body, studying it with a cool thoroughness that disordered every pulse. 'I fell asleep straight after my shower . . .'

'I know.'

The laconic statement brought her head round, her eyes widening as they met his.

'I came up to see if you were all right when I got in,' he told her, answering her unspoken question. 'Margarita was concerned because you never turned up for dinner. You were deeply asleep, wrapped in a damp towel.'

She flushed to the roots of her hair, remembering how she had woken up, knowing that Ben must have seen her like that, must indeed have been the author of her being like that.

'You're blushing.' He stood up and leaned back against the door, indolently at ease, the action emphasising the taut muscles of his thighs. 'Why? You can't be ashamed of your body—it's very beautiful.'

'I'm not. It's just that, like anyone else, I don't like the thought of anyone . . . anyone . . .'

'Seeing it? What a contradiction you are!' He moved, his green gaze marking her sudden flinch. 'You're perfectly safe,' he drawled with almost insulting boredom. 'I might have said your body was beautiful, but that doesn't mean I'm stricken by a lust to possess it.' He glanced at his watch.

'Can you be ready in half an hour?'

Nodding, Sarah turned her attention back to the mirror and her hair, trying to blot out the disturbance caused by his appearance. Today they were filming her meeting with Alain de Courcy; her first since her marriage, and he had come to tell her that Richard had managed to regain her dowry from her brother-in-law Tancred and that she was free to leave the castle where Tancred had virtually imprisoned her and join Richard, who was en route for the Crusade.

'Ben?'

He stopped by the door and watched her. 'Last night I heard you typing. Surely you have a secretary who could do that sort of work?'

'Such wifely concern? Or was Margarita right and you're finding your bed cold and lonely? Save your concern for Dale, Sarah,' he told her harshly. 'Unless he pulls himself together he's going to need it!'

They reached the studio just after half past five. Sarah went straight to Wardrobe, immersing herself in her role as she was dressed in the thin gauzy silks of her costume, her hair hidden beneath the misty draperies of her veil.

She was a woman who had been married against her will to a man she loathed; a man she could not even respect; whose vices and affairs were notorious; a man whose death should have freed her to return to her family had it not been for the machinations of his half-brother who had refused to allow her to return home and who had, moreover, stolen her dowry. But now her brother

had arrived, and Richard's fiery Plantagenet
temperament would no more accept Tancred's
cupidity than did her own, and she lived hourly in
expectation of seeing her brother . . . her favourite
brother . . .

Silk cushions were strewn over the set, incense
burning aromatically, her servants and women
dressed in brilliantly hued silks, the colours all
chosen to complement and emphasise her own
shimmering silvered green. Offset she saw Ben nod
to the cameras and her mouth went dry with
tension. She was Joanna, supposedly, and yet she
felt nothing, her senses too magnetised by the man
watching her. How would she feel if this was her
and she had suddenly discovered she had another
chance of happiness with Ben? She took a deep
breath, no longer afraid. A shrill clarion of
trumpets announced the arrival of Richard's envoy
and she turned, smiling regally, regality giving way
to disbelief and then joy as Paul strode towards
her, causing muted panic and a flurry of silks
among her attendants.

'All right, that's it.' From the set Sarah watched
Ben massage the back of his neck, and behind him
someone said laconically, 'You heard the man—
can it.'

'Sarah, that was marvellous!' Eva praised
warmly. 'Wasn't it, Ben?' She hadn't realised Ben
was at her side, and shivered a little, wondering
how he had moved so silently without her noticing
it, when he was constantly in her thoughts.

'Sarah always was a good actress,' he agreed,
but in a voice more underlined with contempt than
praise, and she had to bite back the impulse to

throw in his face that only by pretending *he* was Paul had she been able to invest it with emotion and desire.

It had been like that with *Shakespeare*. She hadn't needed to pretend when they did their love scene; everything had been all too real.

'You were super, sweetling!'

Why had she never noticed before how insincere Dale could be? She moved slightly as he put his arm round her. 'What's the matter? Oh, I get it. I'm still not forgiven for the other night, is that it?' Out of the corner of her eye Sarah saw Ben's face tighten and then he moved away, his glance scathing as it ripped through her defences. 'How about having dinner with me so that I can apologise in style?' He was talking like someone out of his own films, Sarah thought in detached contempt, unable to understand why, suddenly, she should see him like this. Had *he* changed, or had she?

'No, thanks, Dale. I'm whacked.'

'Are you?' His eyes were glittering as they moved over her face, and just for a second it was like coming face to face with a stranger. Fear ran icily along her spine, and she had wondered why she had never noticed before the vain egotism underlying the charming exterior. 'Or are you hoping to catch a bigger fish? You're still in love with him, aren't you, Sarah? That's why you never told me you were still married. You're wasting your time,' he told her brutally. 'He might want you, but he'll never be able to bring himself to take you knowing you are my leavings.' He said it with such a savage satisfaction that for a moment Sarah was breathless.

'You hate him.' She said it wonderingly, more concerned with her own discovery than his admission of it, startled when Dale responded thickly:

'Damn you, yes! *I* should have been the one who got rave reviews for *Shakespeare*, but I didn't—and why? Because some stupid, big-eyed kid had to go and fall for him and turn him into one of the screen's hottest lovers. I could have killed you for that, Sarah!' He stormed away before she could protest, leaving her feeling as though the world had suddenly turned oddly on its axis. Why had she never realised before the depth of his jealousy of Ben? That he might be jealous had simply never crossed her mind. She had trusted him . . . And he had protected her when Ben . . . Unable to bear the pressure of her thoughts, she went to get dressed, frowning when she discovered she could not find her ring. She had taken off her wedding ring for the filming, and now she stared round, wondering where it could have gone. It didn't have sufficient commercial value for anyone to steal it, but to her its sentimental value was beyond worth. Losing it was like admitting that her marriage was a sham, a deep rending pain that made her draw in her breath on a sharply protesting 'No!'

She spent half an hour looking for it before conceding that it was irrevocably lost, and when she emerged from her dressing room she found Ben waiting for her outside.

'Nice piece of work today, Sarah.' She opened her mouth, startled, as Dale suddenly appeared, nothing about his voice or mien indicative of their last encounter. 'You should give her something a

bit more meaty, Ben; a love scene, she's always
been extra good at those.'

'We're trying to piece together a realistic
reconstruction of the facts, not film soft porn,' Ben
interceded cuttingly.

Sarah started to shiver, her voice tight with fear
as she protested huskily, 'I don't do explicit love
scenes, my agent has instructions to refuse any
scripts that include them—I loathe them!' Her
voice was so vehement that neither of the two men
listening could doubt that she meant what she was
saying.

Dale spoke first, his smile openly triumphant as
he said to Ben, 'That puts you and me in a league
all of our own, doesn't it?' Adding to Sarah,
'Don't forget, sweetling, the offer for tonight still
stands.'

Half an hour later she saw him leaving with
Gina Frey, and wondered at her own malice when
she decided they were well suited to one another.

'Jealous?' She didn't have to turn her head to
know that Ben was taunting her. 'You should
know him well enough by now to know that if he
can't have you he'll soon find someone else—but
remember, Sarah, as long as we're preserving this
fiction of our reconciliation, I won't have you
going to him.'

Sarah ignored him, knowing it would do her no
good to protest her lack of interest in Dale. She
was still suffering from the shock of discovering
another man behind the mask he had always worn
for her; still trying to assess where her instincts
and intuitions had failed her, allowing her to be
deceived into thinking that his concern had all

been for her. Oh, he had protected her from Ben, but only for his own ends, only because of his own jealousy. She shivered suddenly, wondering how much of that jealousy sprang from the fact that Ben had won their bet. At the time, Dale had professed disgust and shame that it had ever been initiated, but how much of that disgust and shame had been real, and how much the actor's skilled camouflage of real feelings?

'Tired?' It was the nearest thing to concern she had ever heard in Ben's voice and she had to blink fiercely against weak tears.

'A little,' she agreed. 'I suppose I'm still suffering from jet-lag.'

'No filming tomorrow, you'll be able to get some rest. It's Sunday,' Ben reminded her dryly, seeing her surprised expression. 'The rest of the cast and crew would probably lynch me if I suggested anything else!'

CHAPTER EIGHT

'MORE coffee? Waffles?'

Sighing her satisfaction, Sarah shook her head. She had never imagined it would be possible for her to feel so lazy. It was eleven o'clock, and she was only just having her breakfast. The sun glinted invitingly on the pool beyond the patio, and yet, she acknowledged, if she did swim, it would probably be in the ocean. She smiled at her own absurdity. She had never totally got over the childhood feeling that no holiday was complete without sea and sand, and since today was virtually a holiday, and she had both on her doorstep, so to speak, she felt almost duty bound to take advantage of them. She sipped her coffee, frowning as she noticed the naked look of her left hand. She had woken a couple of times during the night missing the weight of her wedding ring, or was what she had been missing the totally foolish but now admitted feeling she had always had, that as long as she had worn Ben's ring they were still linked?

'You going sunbathing?' Margarita enquired when she came out to clear the table, glancing speculatively at Sarah's pale skin.

Sarah shook her head. 'I don't tan,' she told her with a smile, 'but I probably will go down to the beach and swim. Is the water safe?'

'Sure, but why not use the pool?' Margarita queried.

'Oh, no reason.' Somehow Sarah felt reluctant

to explain her childish desire to swim in the sea;
perhaps walk along the sand dodging the waves
and investigate any hopeful-looking rock pools. As
a child, how she had hoped against hope to see a
fish! She had always been attracted by water, she
acknowledged, drawn to it in a way she suspected
most children were. And why not? The human
body was largely comprised of it; the oceans of the
world still possessed an aura of mystery, and
terrifying power, the elemental ebb and flow of
their tide echoing the beat of human life.

'Have you seen ... my husband?' Sarah
ventured, wondering if Ben had gone out.

Margarita shrugged. 'Sure. He had his breakfast
about seven and then he disappeared into his
study. I wouldn't disturb him if I were you. He's
probably writing.'

Writing? Guessing that Margarita meant that
Ben was working, and still not sure enough of the
sometimes confusing American usage of familiar
English words, Sarah thanked her for her
breakfast and went back to her room to change
out of her skirt and blouse into a bikini, taking
care to smother her skin in sunscreen and let it
sink in before she pulled a towelling all-in-one
shorts-suit over it. If she did swim she would have
to be careful not to lie too long on the beach
afterwards. The salt water would undoubtedly
wash away the protective barrier of the cream and
she had no desire to burn. As she picked up her
towel her eyes were caught by the sun-hat Ben had
bought her in Spain. Her fingers trembling, she
picked it up. Was she really so badly affected that
merely to *touch* something he had given her made

her like this, her stomach churning and her body weak with need?

The beach on closer inspection proved even more delightful than she had supposed. The ocean had originally formed it by wearing away the softer rock and now the small beach was protected by two arms of harder granite stretching out into the Pacific ensuring strict privacy. As she had walked down through the close-planted shrubs and flowers, their varying scents had been wafted to her, the heat-laden air redolent with their mingled perfumes, bees humming lazily and clumsily from plant to plant.

On the shore the sea had receded, leaving a band of pristine wet sand, and Sarah walked along it, turning to view her own footprints, wondering angrily at the sense of desolation and loneliness that suddenly swept her, catching her breath on a gasp as she saw the silver sparkle of sea spray, and the upward curve of an arm, followed by the dark shape of Ben's head, his hair wetly plastered to his skull, the powerful crawl that propelled him through the water revealing the tautly brown skin of his back and shoulder, reminding her of her suspicion that he sunbathed nude. He had seen her, and was treading water as he found his depth, wading strongly ashore, her eyes riveted to his body, watching the play of muscles beneath his skin, the taut power of his shoulders as he lifted his hands to push back his hair and wipe the moisture from his face. He was watching her too, and suddenly she started to tremble, helplessly transfixed as he came on. His body was beautifully proportioned, not distorted with over-developed

muscles, his skin gleaming beneath the hot caress
of the sun, the salt water following the arrowing
course of the newly slicked body hair disappearing
into the water which lapped just below his navel.

Like someone trapped in a dream Sarah
watched him come on, emerging from the water
like some mythical god, or so it seemed to her
bemused brain, her eyes following his progress,
noting the tautly sleek and tanned skin which
sheathed his muscles and the total difference of his
male shape when compared mentally to hers, his
obvious indifference to his nudity.

Suddenly the dream spell broke, the pounding
of the surf echoed by the heavy thud of her own
heart; panic; a primeval sense of fear, and a
desperate need to escape the intimacy of the
secluded cove ran through her body like fire,
disregarding the sharp sound of her name on Ben's
lips she started to run, blindly, not knowing why
she was running or where, propelled by some
nameless instinct; some frisson of awareness
triggered off by the sight of Ben. She could hear
him behind her; she could almost feel the heat of
his breath against her skin, but still she ran, her
feet entangled in the gritty silk of the sand, the
impact of Ben's arms reaching out to imprison her,
driving out her gasped breath, her body falling
helplessly on to the sand, taking Ben's with it, only
his quick twist saving her from taking his full
weight, her body jarred nevertheless by the
suddenness of her fall.

'Why did you run?'

Ben's voice seemed to reach her from far away,
her whole body trembling with nervous reaction.

Her lips felt dry, and she licked them, tasting the salt, feeling the hectic pound of her heart, trying to move surreptitiously away, feeling Ben's fingers bite into her waist as she did.

She started to struggle, impelled to do so as much by her own treacherous need as by the desire she could see glinting from Ben's eyes, darkening as he resisted her struggles, pinning her to the sand beneath him and securing her there with the weight of his thigh, his chest barely moving while her breath was coming in short jerky gasps, her eyes dilating in sudden shock at the intimate contact of his body. His thigh was roughened by dark hairs, rubbing harshly against the softness of her as she arched desperately to try and throw him off, their eyes locked in a bitter duel, until her sudden desperate movement drew his to the upward thrust of her breasts in their thin covering of cotton. Both of them went still. Sarah could almost feel the insidious beat of her own pulses, her stillness that of the captured, Ben's that of the captor, each infused with subtle innuendo.

It was possible for a man and woman to know of their attraction for one another without so much as a word, if one knew how to read their body signals, or so Sarah had read, and she wondered if Ben could read in hers, all that she was trying so desperately to hide. She should never have run from him, because to do so had surely incited the desire she could feel beating up alongside his anger. It was there in the burning fixity of his glance as it rested on her breasts; in the taut power of his thigh pressing her into the sand. He shifted slightly, balancing himself as he reached deftly behind her, unsnapping the plastic fastening of her bikini top, the sudden shift in his weight revealing his arousal and desire, not a word spoken as he rolled over, taking her with him, her body imprisoned against his, her bikini top sliding away as he tugged it until her nipples brushed against his chest, their involuntary response increasing his arousal, his hands moving down her body, following the line of her spine, the rounded curves of her bottom, holding her until every inch of her was aware of his desire, kissing her, sliding the hot potency of his mouth along her skin, teasing and tormenting, until she was ready to give him anything, if only he would appease the throbbing ache consuming her.

When his fingers tugged at the tiny bows securing her bikini briefs she was far beyond any rational protest. The brief scrap of cotton had long since become an intolerable barrier between them, and when he tugged it, muttering his pleasure into her throat, her body shivered violently in response.

'It feels so good,' he muttered thickly, 'to have all of you against me.' Sarah felt him moving, rolling her down on to her side, her eyes opening to the emerald brilliance of his as he held her a little away from him, studying the pale silk of her skin, now dusted with sand, starting at her toes, which curled protestingly into the sand under his intimate exploration, then moving upwards until her body quivered helplessly beneath a rising tide of desire. He touched his lips to her breasts, first one and then the other, as though unable to resist bestowing the brief caress, his throat beaded with perspiration, the skin tightening on a convulsive swallow as he lifted his head and slid his hands into her hair, his lips just touching hers and then lifting, returning time and time again in the briefly unsatisfying kisses that had her aching for so much more, her head moving protestingly from side to side each time her mouth was tormented, her fingers catching in the black silk of his hair as restraint was abandoned and she clung to him, murmuring her protest against his skin, exulting in the fierce tension of his body as her hands touched it, his mouth opening over hers with hotly demanding urgency. Spiralling waves of pleasure thudded through her, culminating in a desire so intense it seemed impossible to endure. Every time he touched her she wanted him more, and now her body wasn't prepared to be denied any more.

When he released her mouth Ben was breathing as hard as if he had been running, his chest rising and falling with the effort of it, his head tipped back, and his eyes closed, his hands sliding possessively to cover her breasts, his body shuddering as his thumbs investigated their aroused fullness, his touch making her arch hungrily against him, her hands moving down to his waist, impelled by her aching urgency to move lower until he tensed and muttered, pushing her back on the sand, his hands exploring every inch of her, knowing just how and where to stroke and caress her, slowly driving her far beyond the point where she was conscious of anything other than his mastery of her body and his knowledge of all its secrets. Her fingertips grazed the tender skin of his stomach, making him shudder wrenchingly, holding her off so that she could see the dully

hectic colour reddening his cheek bones, and the
febrile glitter of his eyes, his whole body tense as
she touched her lips to the skin so recently
explored by her fingers, her insides turning weak
with molten delight at the discovery of his own
vulnerability; the hoarse cry he wasn't quite able
to suppress as her lips moved lower; the biting
strength in the arms that suddenly gripped and
lifted her. Her body clenched in fierce pleasure as
his mouth dropped to her breasts, exploring the
deep cleft between them, until with a thick
exclamation his fingers curved possessively around
their swollen fullness, his lips moving provocatively
from one to the other until his body was hard and
thrusting against her, and he was holding her so
tightly that she could feel the erotic drag of his
teeth against her skin, their breathing mutually
laboured and uneven.

The shrill sound that cut across it stiffened
Sarah into stunned shock. Dimly she was aware of
Ben swearing as he rolled away, his voice thick
and unsteady as he told her, 'Telephone, and if I
don't go and answer it soon, someone's going to
come down here looking for me, and there's no
way I want anyone else to see you looking like
that.' His eyes skimmed the shape of her body,
watching the delicate flush of colour staining her
skin as Sarah became aware of her betraying
arousal, and then to her surprise Ben reached for
her and kissed her hard although unsatisfyingly on
the mouth. 'That's just to remind you that we've
got unfinished business for later.' He stood up,
reaching for her towel, saying with a grin, 'I'm not
particularly prudish, but I don't think it would be

wise to bump into Margarita in my present state!'
and laughed as she coloured richly and started
scrambling into her own clothes.

By the time she was dressed he was already at
the top of the steps. She made no haste to hurry
after him. If he had a phone call there was not
much point, and as she made her way slowly up
the steps, her body still languorous with pleasure,
she shivered in anticipation of the promise implicit
in his last words. Did they mean he had forgiven
her? Or simply that his desire for her was so great
that it overruled everything else?

'It was Gina inviting us over,' Ben told her,
coming out on to the patio as she crossed it. 'She's
having a barbecue, and little though I want to go I
feel on this occasion it might be . . . politic . . .'

Because he resented what might happen if they
remained alone? Did that mean he was already
regretting his words on the beach? Since she didn't
feel able to ask him, Sarah simply inclined her
head, hoping her voice sounded indifferently
steady as she said evenly, 'In that case I'd better go
and get changed. What sort of thing ought I to
wear?'

'Ordinarily I'd say jeans and a tee-shirt, but
knowing Gina she'll be doing things in style—
probably with Pucci silks!'

They weren't something Sarah possessed, but
she did have some silk trousers with a matching
jacket, in a pale cream. She had bought them in a
sale, getting them because they were such a small
size, and had been lucky enough to buy with them
a cream camisole top embroidered in rich pinks
and lilacs. The suit looked good on her, she knew,

her hair floating on her shoulders, her feet bare in strappy kid sandals, her make-up deliberately brief, knowing that she would find it next to impossible to keep it on in the heat. As a precaution she picked up her bikini and rolled it up in a towelling robe. There might be swimming, and if there was she didn't want to be obliged to borrow anything of Gina's, so instinctive and deeply felt was her dislike of the other woman.

Ben's silent appreciation when she descended the stairs brought faint colour to her skin, and her chin lifted warily, until she realised he was smiling.

'I've just realised how often you do that,' he commented thoughtfully, watching her with narrowed eyes. 'Every time you feel threatened in the slightest way, your chin lifts.'

'Perhaps because someone once told me you should take all life's blows on it,' Sarah joked, wishing he was less perceptive. She wasn't ready yet to have him know every last intimate thing about her, able to judge her moods and feelings. Today he had unbent towards her, but she wasn't sure how long that would last; or ir indeed he really meant it. She wasn't naïve enough to believe that simply because a man desired her it meant happy ever after, but at least it was a step in the right direction, a more optimistic inner voice crowed. And they were married. Who knew what the future might hold?

She spent the drive to Gina's indulging in the most satisfying of daydreams, her mouth curved in a softly tender smile, unaware of the looks Ben darted her when his attention wasn't on the road.

'Here we are.' She came down to earth with a

bump as he turned the car into Gina's drive. Unlike Ben's house Gina's wasn't secluded, but one of many along what was all the same a most exclusive and elegant road.

A crowd of people, including some faces she recognised, were gathered round the pool, the majority of the women dressed as Ben had predicted in expensive couture play-clothes. Accepting a drink from one of the waiters, Sarah studied her surroundings. They were everything she had imagined Hollywood to be—and dreaded—expensive, soulless and somehow a fitting background for a woman like Gina. But it would never suit her; she wanted a home; not necessarily as large as Ben's, but a home nevertheless where she could bring up a family. A giant hand squeezed her heart. Children. Ben's children—God, how she ached to bear them! The primitiveness of her own response amazed her. She had always known that she liked children, but never that she would feel this earthy sensual need to have her body ripen with a man's seed, his child growing within her.

'Ah, darling, there you are.' Sarah was ignored as Gina swept Ben up into the crowd surrounding her. Not wanting to seem clinging, she turned back to study the view, wondering if Gina shared the house with her lover, or owned it in her own right.

'Sarah!' She hadn't heard Dale approach and she didn't smile. 'You're angry.' His voice held wry self-remorse. 'I suppose I deserve it. Look, could you try and forget what I said at the studio? My only excuse is that I'm off my head with jealousy. I always did envy Ben you, but never as much as I do now. Will you forgive me, Sarah?'

She didn't want to, but to do so was easier than prolonging the interview. 'We ought to talk,' he added softly, grasping her hand. 'Come on, we'll go inside.' She couldn't release his grip of her fingers and short of making a scene there was little she could do. He seemed to know exactly where he was going, although Sarah was dismayed to be dragged into a ground floor bedroom, its windows open to the pool area.

'Sweetling, I'm so sorry.' Dale's voice was huskily urgent. 'Can't we kiss and make up?' His hands grasping her upper arms, his mouth probing the unyielding line of hers as Sarah fought silently against his kiss, angry enough to want to tear herself out of his arms, but unwilling to provoke a further scene by doing so.

'Oh, darling, I'm sure you can't have seen them come in here. It's a bedroom!'

Sarah froze in panic as she heard Gina's voice outside, her footsteps accompanied by a heavier masculine tread. The door was pushed open, her scream of fright silenced as Dale thrust her down on the bed, and turned quickly, his face expressing the full gamut of guilt and defiance as he stared upwards towards Ben.

Sarah wanted to cover her eyes, to die quickly and painlessly, but the look in Ben's eyes promised that she would do neither. She sat up, words of explanation tumbling from her lips, but Dale beat her to it, perfidious, jealous Dale who was even now holding out a shiny gold ring, his voice sorrowful, belying the mocking cruelty in his eyes as he handed it to her. 'You'd better take this, sweetling. You left it in my shower.'

Sarah felt as though she were taking part in a horrendous play. Ben, Dale and Gina were all watching her with varying expressions, Dale's triumphantly cruel, Gina's all spite and malice, and Ben's—dear God, how could she endure the look in Ben's eyes! It stripped her of all her defences, laid her wide open to the searing contempt of his bitter glance. It was pointless trying to defend herself and so she didn't bother, but struggled to sit up, wondering numbly what was going to happen.

'Come on, Ben, you've always known the score.' That was Dale, letting his triumph show, only Ben wasn't to know why he was triumphant. He assumed it was because she and Dale were lovers.

'Perhaps I've been listening to another tune.' That was Ben, his voice flat and almost defeated, hardening slowly as he added, harshly, 'It seems you have a natural propensity for bedroom scenes, Sarah, and as a director I'd be a fool if I didn't make use of such a God-given talent. Seeing that you haven't been at any pains to hide your ... affair from the eyes of the world, you won't have any objection to my changing some of your final love scene, making it a little more explicit. That's what you recommended, wasn't it, Dale? And if he doesn't mind then why the hell should I?' Ben finished thickly. 'Let's see you display your natural aptitude between the sheets where it does any actress the most good—up on the screen!'

'No!' What should have been a shout was a husky croak of denial, and horror flitted darkly over her features as she stared up at the silent trio. 'You can't do that, Ben,' she husked defiantly.

'You can't just change the script like that! You'll need to get the permission of the writer, and then there's the re-writing of the script, and the backers . . .'

'The backers wanted a hot love scene in the film all along,' Ben told her ruthlessly. 'They'll be over the moon—and don't even think of trying to break your contract, or the studio will break you.' Sarah knew his threat was all too real, and shuddered in real anguish. She couldn't play a heavy love scene. She *couldn't*! She struggled upwards, panting, clutching at straws, repeating shakily, 'You can't do it, Ben. You'll never get the writer's permission, the script is perfect as it is, he won't let you butcher it simply to torment me . . .'

Gina's jeering laughter filled the silence. 'You little fool,' she scoffed, 'who do you think wrote it? Hasn't he even told you that much? Well, go on, darling,' she urged Ben triumphantly, 'tell your stupid little wife exactly who is the writer she so blatantly hero-worships, and exactly why you can alter the script if you wish.' Without giving Ben a chance to respond, she turned on Sarah, her eyes glittering with dislike. 'Ben wrote the film,' she told her. 'Everyone connected with the film knew that. All but you. Some reconciliation! Ben obviously didn't have much faith in it succeeding. I suppose he didn't tell you because he didn't want you filing a hefty claim for alimony. Your husband's an extremely wealthy man, and he can do just what he likes with this film, sweetie—and with you. He owns fifty per cent of the studio!'

Sarah lay limply on the bed, her eyes burning

with horror and pain, pleading with Ben to deny Gina's assertions.

'It's true?' Her voice was a broken whisper, her pride irreparably broken as two painful tears welled up in her eyes and ran unchecked down her face, her body feeling as though it had been physically beaten, real sickness tasting sour in her mouth. Ben was that man whom she had secretly so much admired; Ben had written that hauntingly emotive script, Ben who had never shown her an ounce of the compassion he had given so liberally to his characters.

'Come on, Sarah, we're going home.' Strangely enough, of the trio he was the only one who evinced no signs of triumph, his hands cool and firm on her body as he pulled her upright.

'Home?' Sarah spat the word hysterically. 'You honestly expect me to go back with you after this?'

'You'd better believe it.' His voice was coldly emphatic, and Gina shivered sensually, cooing, 'Darling, you sound so masculine! Such a turn-on to find a really strong man!'

Strong! He was made of ... of ... ice, Sarah thought bitterly. 'I'm not coming with you.'

'Oh yes, you are.' He bent swiftly and scooped her up into his arms, shouldering his way past Dale and out of the door. They emerged from the side at a side entrance close to where the cars were parked, and Ben dumped her unceremoniously in his.

'I haven't come this far with the film to have it all ruined now by you. You're not pulling out now, Sarah,' he warned her. 'I've got too much at stake.'

'Then don't make me do this love scene—I can't, Ben!' God, how she hated herself for pleading, her mind writhed in torment, but anything was better than having to endure such an ordeal.

He paused, turning to her, his eyes merciless in their scrutiny. 'Why is it you hate them so much? It doesn't matter,' he told her curtly before she could reply. 'Perhaps the fact that you do is revenge enough. You think it strange that I should feel a need for revenge?' His mouth curled disdainfully. 'It is a little theatrical, I agree, but sometimes all of us need to seek pride's appeasement, and for what you've done to mine I could cheerfully consign you to the fires of hell itself. So you will do this scene, is that understood?'

Numbly Sarah sat in the seat, still unable to take it all in. *Ben* had written the script! That explained the typewriter and the constant use he made of it. Obviously he was now working on something else. Frantically she contemplated running away, letting Carew sort out her breaking of the contract when she got home, but Ben had her passport. She was trapped, trapped like a gazelle beneath the lion's paw, and her mind circled crazily in terror trying to find a way out.

CHAPTER NINE

IT was unthinkable that Sarah could sleep. Her first wild impulse on returning to the house was to ring Carew and beg him to find some way of releasing her from her contract; she no longer even cared that it would mean that she lost the role of a lifetime. She could not. She *would* not play out an explicit love scene, watched and bullied by Ben. Fear made her brain a tight ball of pain inside her skull. Ben had assessed her horrified response to the threat of such a love scene with a bitter triumph that warned her that he would do his utmost to exact retribution from her, drop by excruciating drop. There would be no compassion; no kindness shown to her. He probably wouldn't even allow them to have a closed set. Lifting her hot face from her pillow, she listened, catching the faint sound of someone typing, her heart thudding painfully against her chest wall. Ben was working. Re-writing her love scene? She wanted to go down and beg him to reconsider, explain to him that . . .

That she loved him and had done all along; that Dale had never been her lover, no matter how much he might have tried to make it look otherwise? Even if she were given a written guarantee that by doing so Ben would believe her she didn't have the courage to admit her feelings to him. She would be shown none of the compassion that came across so strongly in the film.

Two long and wearisome days crawled by when she never saw Ben, but heard the constant rattle of the typewriter keys through the closed study door. Filming had been suspended, and although Paul had telephoned and offered to take her out, Sarah had refused. 'I believe Ben is writing us a steamy love scene,' Paul commented before he hung up. 'I must say I'm surprised. From the way he looked at me when I kissed you, I thought he was tempted to cut the romance between us out altogether!' When Paul rang off, Sarah leaned back against the wall, replacing the receiver with fingers that shook so badly she had to use both hands, her teeth biting deep into her lower lip as she fought not to make a sound. She heard Margarita walk into the hall and was aware of the concerned look she gave her, but only in a vague way as though a clear plastic bubble separated her from the rest of mankind, and that only her pain was real.

On the third morning after Ben had found her in Gina's bedroom with Dale, Sarah was walking along the beach. She came down to it a good deal, drawn by the solitude and the hypnotic pounding of the surf against the sand, the sound vaguely comforting. Almost she was tempted to simply walk into the ocean until it wasn't possible to walk any more; to give herself up to its dark enchantment and allow it to steal away her breath and her life, but the same small flame of courage which had refused to allow her to deny her love for Ben kept her eyes fixed firmly on the horizon rather than the seductive drag of the tide, as she forced herself to remember time and time again how Ben had made love to her on this very beach;

how she had given herself up to him, and how she
had even begun to hope that somehow they might
find a way to ... to love one another, she
admitted, her face a bitter mask of pain for her
naïve folly.

When she heard Ben calling her from the top of
the steps her first impulse was to run. But to
where? Trying to suppress the nervous agitation
churning her stomach, she started to climb the
steps, her feet dragging. At the top Ben was
waiting for her, leaning back against the wall, the
breeze flattening the thin silk shirt he was wearing
to the hard breadth of his chest, tight, dark jeans
outlining the masculine thrust of his thighs.

'Not contemplating drowning yourself, I trust?'
he mocked as she reached him. 'You won't escape
me that way, Sarah,' he added savagely. 'I'd fight
like ten demons to keep you in this world, on this
side of the hereafter ...'

'So that you can torment and punish me?' Sarah
managed, shivering in helpless response. 'What
kind of man are you, Ben?' she choked unsteadily.
'What kind of pleasure do you get from doing this
to me?'

'A kind you wouldn't begin to understand,' he
assured her brutally. 'You're far too shallow.
Now, I've finished the alterations. I want you to
come and read them.' She looked up and instantly
felt sick when she saw the green glitter of his eyes
beneath the downcast black lashes. Outwardly he
was completely calm, but underneath ... Sarah
shuddered. His body seemed to emanate an
intensity of anger that curled tight fingers of
tension along her spine, her eyes unable to resist

the magnetic pull of his as she found herself allowing him to propel her back into the house, and through the hall where he paused by the telephone and demanded suddenly, 'Who telephoned you this morning? Dale?'

'As a matter of fact it was Paul.' She tried to sound aloof and disdainful, her voice coolly clear. 'He's heard that you're changing our love scene.'

'And he objects?' Ben's mouth curled. 'Don't try that one on me, Sarah. He'll be thanking his lucky stars. A scene like the one we did on *Shakespeare* could make him the hottest box office property around, especially when it's played with you . . . I know what it did for my career.'

He was goading her deliberately, baiting her and waiting for her response. He wanted her to lose her temper, Sarah could sense that, and because she could she deliberately refused to let her mind comprehend his insults, simply pinning a blank look on her face and waiting for him to open the study door.

'You can keep your cool now,' Ben murmured as he bent to turn the handle, 'but how long for? I saw your face when I told you I was altering the love scene—remember?'

'I'm not stupid, Ben,' Sarah retorted evenly. 'I know you're doing this to hurt me. What I don't understand is why.'

'You know why well enough——' Ben argued tersely, '—finding you like that with Dale . . .'

Sarah felt as though she were gripped in some painfully numbing cold. Had she ever known this man to whom she was married? He would destroy her—there was no other word to describe what he planned—and he would do it simply to salve his wounded pride.

'Sit down.' Ben thrust her down into a chair, without waiting for her response, then went over to the typewriter and riffling through some papers while Sarah looked around and tried to steady her pounding heart. The room was utilitarian rather than glamorous, one wall bookshelved and stacked with books, the room furnished with two desks and half a dozen or so filing cabinets.

'Here.' Ben passed her a sheaf of typewritten pages. 'You'll have to excuse my typing errors,' he added mockingly, 'but I'm sure you'll get the drift.'

Slowly, hardly daring to let her eyes rest on the paper, Sarah glanced down. At first the typing danced illegibly before her eyes, and she realised to her horror that her eyes were full of tears. It was several seconds before she could blink them away sufficiently to enable her to read, her knuckles white with the effort of keeping her hands steady as she did.

She had barely read one page when she let the papers fall, her face white with pain and disbelief.

'I can't do this, Ben,' she told him defiantly, every muscle tensed to back up her refusal. 'I can't . . .'

'Oh, come on, Sarah,' he drawled smoothly, bending to gather the scattered sheets and re-stacking them. 'What's all the fuss about? All you have to do is simply go to your lover and beg him to make love to you. Where is the difficulty in that? Dale tells me it's something you're very good at,' he added with insulting ease, giving her a smile that made her skin crawl. 'Now come on, read the rest.'

There was no way she was going to be allowed to escape. Slowly and bitterly she read on, her body growing a little colder and emptier with each line as she saw the explicit detail Ben had written into the script.

If she was simply reading the passage in a book she might find it powerfully erotic; she might even identify herself with Joanna, but to actually act out what Ben had written!

'We start shooting tomorrow,' he added blandly, watching her face for signs of betrayal. 'For this one I think we'll have a rehearsal. Full cast and crew, I want to get the feel of their reaction . . .'

Glancing into his face, Sarah allowed her lips to close over any plea for a closed set. He would love her to beg, and then to refuse her, she thought bitterly—well, from somewhere she would find the courage and the will-power to go through with this scene, and no matter what it cost her she would not betray to him by so much as a quiver what she was really feeling.

'Umm, I think that's okay.' Linda paused before studying Sarah's costume. The entire set seemed to quiver with anticipation over the filming of the love scene, a subtle tension infusing cast and crew alike. Sarah was wearing the boy's garments she had borrowed from Richard's page to enable her to walk through the camp unnoticed on her way to see her lover, Richard just having told her that she was to marry Raymond of Toulouse.

Beyond her line of vision Sarah knew Props

were preparing the set; the mock-up of her lover's pavilion. Initially the scene was to be played as before, only instead of immediately recognising her despite her page's disguise, this time Paul was to mistake her for a page and to command her to assist him bathe. This part of the scene she could probably endure, but she was dreading what would follow; her plea to her lover to make love to her and then their abandoned lovemaking which would follow.

'Sarah, are you ready?'

Ben! Sarah closed her eyes. He wouldn't stop hounding her. Sometimes she thought he had a Machiavellian talent for discovering her weak spots, pounding mercilessly at them until ... Until what? Until she was totally destroyed? Shivering slightly, she walked slowly towards the set, forcing herself to exclude everything but her role. If she could just do that she might have a chance.

'Now, remember,' Ben instructed when she reached him, 'this is your only chance to be with your lover; what happens now must last a lifetime; you're a woman, not a child, initially you are the more powerful of the two. And Paul,' he continued, beckoning the actor over, 'at first you simply follow Sarah's lead. You love her, but you're Richard's knight and you know of his plans for her, but you're also a man, and she's a woman you've loved and desired and now she's in your bed, yet part of you resents her for coming to you. I want this love scene to have the raw explosive impact Richard's do not. There must be an element of conflict in it as well as ultimately love. Okay?'

Willing herself to close her mind to everything
else, Sarah took her place, waiting for the cue that
had her lifting back the flap of the pavilion and
walking inside. Paul's non-recognition of her, his
curt instruction to help him undress and bathe, all
went well. She even managed the bit she had been
dreading, where she had to unfasten and remove
her tunic before begging Paul to make love to her
with tolerable aplomb, although her fingers
trembled as she reached for her tunic, her self-
control suddenly faltering, and panic clawing at
her spine until Paul realised what was happening
and ignored the script's instructions that he was to
wait until she was fully undressed before touching
her, and instead picked her up as she stood
shivering and carried her across to the bed.

'Cut!' Ben's voice sliced through the silence.
'That isn't how I want it played, Sarah . . .'

Sarah knew Paul must have felt her tense, her
eyes wide and unseeing like a hunted animal,
fingers curled into her palms. No one else could
see her face because Paul's body hid her head, and
after a quick concerned look at her he called back,
'Ben, it's only a rehearsal, we can put it right when
we actually film.'

No cold voice came to argue against him, and
Sarah felt her tense body relax slightly, aware of
and grateful for Paul's concern as he leaned closer
and asked her, 'Sarah, are you all right? Do you
want me to get Ben?'

'No!' Her voice held sharp terror, and again
Paul frowned, but Ben had already given the signal
for them to continue. Twice Paul had to remind
her of her lines and Sarah knew she had never

given a worse or less convincing performance in her life. Had she been playing a terrified virgin about to be ravished by her captor her responses would have been first-class, but for a deeply sensual woman in the arms of the man she was supposed to love, they were appalling.

'Look, Ben, this just isn't working,' Paul said calmly, when Ben had ordered them to stop for the umpteenth time. 'We're all on edge. Sarah's a bundle of nerves, and I must admit I feel as awkward as hell trying to make love to her with her husband looking on. I know it's all part of an actor's work, but this time, it's just not working. Why don't you close the set, and perhaps it would be better if you stood in for me,' he suggested, shocking Sarah into sick immobility. 'After all, from the back we're much the same, both dark-haired, and they could always edit the rest later.'

Ben had joined them on the set, his eyes boring mercilessly into hers as Sarah tried not to let him see how she felt. 'Would you prefer that, Sarah?' he asked softly.

Her shudder betrayed her, and she knew she should not have let him witness it. It was bad enough enduring this with Paul whom she liked and that was all, but to endure it with Ben, who set her body on fire every time he came near her ... She couldn't do it. But Ben intended to make her do it, she had read that much in his eyes, and there was absolutely nothing she could do to stop him.

She sat shivering while the set was cleared, pretending to read her lines, but in reality trying to

will herself into a state of mind that would enable
her to get through the scene.

'We'll film it this time,' Ben told the camera
crew tersely. 'We've wasted enough time on it
already.'

Although he and Paul were much of a height,
Ben was broader, which meant that the chain mail
was that much harder to remove, Sarah thought
inconsequentially as she struggled to remove it,
willing herself not to think of the body underneath.
Above her Ben was speaking Paul's lines, which
would later be dubbed, his eyes mirroring the
anger he was supposed to feel after learning from
Richard of Joanna's marriage. Undressing Paul
had not produced the same trembling anguish she
was experiencing now, Sarah acknowledged, her
mind beating out the words, 'You're not Sarah,
you're Joanna,' the refrain thudding feverishly
inside her skull as she tried to enact them.

When it came to the part where she had to allow
her hands to linger on Ben's body he had no need
to manufacture his biting anger, Sarah thought
distantly, all the breath shaken out of her as he
grasped her tunic, soaking it, exclaiming, 'God's
blood, boy, do you dare to caress me as though
you were a woman?'

This was the cue for Sarah to reveal herself, and
Ben had made sure that she had to do so in both
senses of the word. A painful tattoo of resentment
thudded inside her head and she managed to
unfasten and remove her hose and tunic as per the
script, not daring to look into Ben's face to see how
he was reacting as she released her hair and let it
swirl round her shoulders in a protective cloak.

'Joanna!'

Ben was still a first-rate actor, a tiny portion of her brain recorded as he stood up and stepped towards her, the word softened with surprise and then hardened with anger.

'By what miracle does the Queen of Sicily deign to honour the tent of a mere knight? Or have you come that I might congratulate you on another marriage? This time my lady is more fortunate. Raymond of Toulouse is neither old nor impotent, and it is well known that my lady comes from a lusty family.'

He waited, knowing that she must come to him, touch him, and, her face pinched with tension, Sarah did, not knowing or caring if she spoke her lines right or wrong, only emerging from the shadowy corners, deep within her mind, where she had hidden when she was on the bed, pinned there by Ben's superior weight, an anger burning up in him which seemed more real than assumed, fires burning deep within her body as his hands stroked over her skin.

Everything that she had feared about this scene rose up inside her to mock her, only her reactions were a thousand times worse than she had expected, because it wasn't Paul who held her, Paul with whom she must re-live the agony of remembrance, but *Ben*; Ben who had taught her body the meaning of love, who had taken her beyond shyness and selfconsciousness to a plane where nothing mattered other than him, and who had drawn from her the performance that had briefly made them both famous, and he was going to do the same thing again; deceiving her body

with his touch, until her desire for him overruled
the cautions of her mind.

His mouth burned against her skin, his gritted,
'And does my lady find my performance satisfac-
tory? Perhaps her husband will give me some fine
lands for it!' barely touching her consciousness,
although the biting tone reached deep down inside
her, touching her where she could still be hurt, the
lash of his scorn drawing tears of blood. Her body
tensed against him, she struggled to recall her
lines, vaguely aware of him touching locked
muscles, stroking them into acquiescence and
acceptance of his touch and weight, the storm of
his anger dying away to be replaced by gentleness
and then desire. And it was the gentleness that
finally betrayed her. It was no use telling her
aching body that it was all false; that Ben was
simply playing a part, because she was already
softening in response, and not just softening, but
responding, Sarah recognised in mounting horror,
her mind desperately trying to withstand the
seduction of his touch. And then she knew!

Ben intended her to respond to him; he wanted
this final humiliation, and he wouldn't stop until
he got it. Balked of humiliating her by forcing her
to go through the love scene in public with Paul,
he had sensed her reaction to him and was playing
on it, using her vulnerability as a weapon against
her, slowly breaking down her resistance, until she
was a trembling, aching bundle of need lying
weightless in his arms, feeling the slow scorch of
his mouth and hands against her skin before the
final tide of desire rushed over her and she clung
helplessly, opening her eyes at his command to let

him see down into the far reaches of her soul. For a moment something seemed to glimmer in his eyes, but then it was gone and he was speaking Paul's lines, jolting her into awareness of how much she had betrayed, and some part of her that was still functioning made her responses, but her voice was a whisper devoid of tone of depth; dead like the rest of her, her body merely a physically functioning shell inside which she had quietly and totally withdrawn.

Somehow she was back in Wardrobe, and Linda and her assistants were helping her to change, Linda's worried glances something she was aware of but too numb to question.

Outside Paul was waiting for her, dressed in a tee-shirt and jeans, frowning as he touched her icy hand. 'Ben's waiting for the rushes. How about a drink and then we'll go and see them.'

'No!' The denial burst inside her like a small volcano, but the sound emerging from her throat was quiet and without vehemence. 'I don't want to see them.'

'Sarah . . .'

'Please, Paul, I don't want to talk about it.' Suddenly she was unutterably tired. All she wanted to do was sleep, and never ever have to wake.

'That was some performance, according to the camera crew.' Dale's sneering voice raised the hairs at the back of her scalp, but she ignored him. 'But then Ben always did know how to get a response out of you, and we both know why.'

'Do we?' Somehow she managed to face him.

'Sure we do. You love him.' His eyes narrowed. 'Do you still love him—after what he's done to you today?'

'I'm no longer capable of loving anyone,' she told him emotionlessly. 'Not loving, nor hating.'

'Liar!' Dale mocked her tauntingly. 'You still love him, Sarah, and you always will.'

Dale was right, Sarah acknowledged tiredly. It seemed she had no pride and no matter what Ben did to her, nothing could kill her love. He had given instructions that no one was to leave the set in case they had to re-shoot, and Sarah sat alone in the canteen, toying with a cold cup of coffee, knowing that she simply could not go through the scene again.

She knew Ben had walked in even without lifting her head by the ripple of speculation running swiftly round the room.

'Paul, Sarah, we're doing the scene again. If you'd both get ready.'

Sarah lifted her head, her eyes dark with fear and pain, noticing vaguely that Ben's hair was untidy as though he had raked angry fingers through it and that his mouth was circled by a taut white line which presaged a savage outburst of anger.

'I won't do it!' Was that really her own voice, so strained and husky? Most of the crew and cast had left the restaurant, drifting back to the set, only Gina and Dale lingering, watching.

'Sarah . . .' That was Paul, and Sarah recognised the note of concern and warning.

'Poor Sarah!' That was Dale, his voice dripping pseudo-sympathy with every malice-tipped word.

'Of course you know why she hates doing love scenes so much, don't you, Ben? It's because the poor thing's so desperately in love with you. That wasn't acting when we filmed *Shakespeare*, and . . .'

Sarah couldn't listen to any more. She turned and ran, her feet skimming the floor, Ben's voice sharply calling her name failing to halt her, only adding to her panic. Ben's car stood in the lot and she slid into it, reaching for the ignition key, shivering as she saw Ben emerge from the canteen and search for her, his head turning sharply as he heard the engine fire. Dale was behind him and Sarah saw him put his hand on Ben's arm, and Ben start to shake it off, before stopping. No doubt Dale was telling him everything. It was his revenge on her because she had dared to prefer Ben, but she no longer cared. Ben knew she loved him, knew of her stupidity, and she felt more naked than she had done when she stood before him on the set and felt him scrutinise her body.

The car had automatic transmission and Sarah had travelled the road to the studio often enough to know the way. She couldn't stay in America any longer now, if Ben wanted to re-film the scene he would have to find another actress. The un-alleviated stress of being so close to him was driving her out of her mind—almost literally, she thought grimly. Any more of this agonising torment and tension and she could well end up in a mental hospital.

She realised she had reached the house and stopping the car jumped out. Her passport, she thought feverishly, she needed her passport. It was

Margarita and Ramón's day off and the house was silent, but not locked. She went straight to Ben's study, opening drawers, searching through them, panic making her clumsy, every movement impelled by a growing sense of urgency. Where was it? Did Ben have a secret safe? Could he have left it at the studio? No, it must be here somewhere . . . She renewed her assault upon the desk drawers.

'Sarah . . .!'

She stiffened. Ben had followed her. She could hear his footsteps in the hall, measured and firm. Her heart thudded suffocatingly, the study was suddenly too confining.

'Sarah, where are you?' She heard him move to the door, watching the handle depress with a horrified fascination before realising she could escape through the patio. The glass door jammed and she tugged at it frenziedly, hearing Ben enter the room behind her, his swift curse bitten off as he saw her. For a second neither of them moved and then Ben glanced at his desk, his jaw clenching in anger as he took a step towards her.

The patio door moved smoothly under her fingers and Sarah was running, her heart thudding frantically against her ribs, knowing Ben wasn't far behind her, careless of which direction she ran in, until Ben's voice made her tense and swing round, trying to get her bearings, shocked to discover that he was less than a yard away; close enough almost to reach out his hand and . . .

'No!' The vehement denial was choked out of her throat and she stepped back instinctively in the same moment that Ben moved, his harsh, 'Sarah, for God's sake, the pool!' ringing numbly in her ears as she slipped and fell backwards through space and then down, down into the embrace of the life-stealing water.

CHAPTER TEN

'You crazy little fool, didn't you hear me shout?' They were standing by the poolside, Sarah shivering and shaking with reaction and shock, dimly aware that Ben had followed her into the pool and dragged her out, his chest rising and falling heavily with the effort of doing so, his hands warm against the cold skin of her waist, chilled by her shock and her soaking clothes.

'It's no good, Ben, I won't do that scene again.' Her voice was ragged with pain, her throat stinging from the water she had swallowed, her hands going up to his chest to push him away, her fingers curling tightly into her palms as he refused to release her, her small fists flailing impotently against his chest.

'Sarah darling, please don't!'

There in the warm huskiness of his voice, the quiet despair and pain underlying the softly spoken words was all she had longed to hear for so many barren years when they had been apart, and Sarah finally knew that her reason must have deserted her. Ben would never speak to her like that! Tears of exhaustion and defeat flooded her eyes. What was he trying to do to her now? Was this some new form of torture his Machiavellian brain had devised? She couldn't endure it!

'All right, all right, it's all true,' she moaned feverishly, 'I do love you—I always did. There was never anyone but you, even when Dale told me about your bet. I should have hated and despised you for that, but I couldn't.'

If she had expected him to deny it she had misjudged him. There was silence and then a pitying, 'Oh, Sarah!' and the pressure of his hands moved from her waist to her back, holding her against him, allowing her to draw strength from his body.

'I can't film that scene again, Ben . . .' Her voice started to rise hysterically. 'I can't . . . I can't!'

'Shush now, it's all right. Let's get you dry.' She was in his arms, her hair curling damply over his arm, her eyes closing as she felt the reassuring beat of his heart beneath her cheek, only surely it was slightly unsteady, perhaps because of her weight. Exhausted by her emotional storm, she was barely aware of being carried into Ben's room until he opened his bathroom door and slid her to her feet, the hands that had held her in his arms quickly stripping off her wet clothes, ignoring her feeble protests, his ministrations not stopping until she was wrapped in a thick fluffy towel. Picking her up again, Ben opened the door, carried her across to his bed and placed her on it, the concern she saw in his eyes making her heartbeats thud.

'Dale was never my lover.'

Now why had she told him that? Her face flamed. What possible interest could it be to Ben who had shared her bed? The downward flick of his lashes so that she could not see his eyes confirmed her thoughts, his slow, 'I know,' startling her into forgetting her despair long enough to stare up at him.

'You do? But . . .'

'Let me get these wet things off and then we'll talk.'

He was gone about five minutes, returning wearing a navy towelling robe, his legs and feet bare beneath the hem, his hair ruffled as though it had been towelled.

'Your hair is soaking,' he told her, reaching out a hand to touch it. 'I'll get a towel.'

He came back and sat on the bed behind her, rubbing briskly at her damp hair, much as though she were a child, then combing gently through its damp length, the gentle tug of the comb and the warm pressure of his hand on her shoulder causing fresh emotions to flare. Dear God, would she never be free of this? Sarah wondered helplessly. Would she always be as vulnerable to his touch as she was now, or would the years to come bring some measure of peace, of indifference? She could only pray that it might be so.

'I've decided to change your love scene with Paul back to its original form.'

He was still sitting behind her, and short of twisting round to look into his face, Sarah had no way of knowing how he felt. She knew she should have felt relief, but somehow she was incapable of feeling any emotion, only a vast, empty nothingness, through which she managed to murmur a dull, 'Thank you.'

'*You're* thanking *me*?' She was twisted round in his arms, her vulnerable emotions subjected to the fierce scrutiny of his glance, his fingers tightening almost painfully on her upper arms. 'Dear God, Sarah!' He leaned his forehead against hers, his eyes closed, the dark lashes lying like twin fans. 'Dear God, Sarah, how you shame me!' His eyes opened, his index finger tracing the shape of her lips, his forehead creasing in a frown as they trembled. 'You must believe me. If I'd had any idea how you felt, I'd never have forced you into that scene.'

'I swore I'd never do another one after *Shakespeare*,' Sarah told him huskily, feeling that his apology deserved some response. 'I knew then that what I was doing wasn't acting, and I hated it when my ... my performance was acclaimed. If it hadn't been with you ... but then you knew that, didn't you?' she asked dully. 'You'd guessed how I felt about you before Dale said anything, otherwise you'd never have known how much it would torture me to have to do that scene with you today.'

She couldn't look at him, although she heard the small explosive sound of the expletive started and then caught back as her chin was gripped and her face turned up to his. 'You thought that?' Ben sounded bitterly incredulous. 'You thought I was callously tormenting you?' He shook his head as though unable to believe what he had heard. 'No, Sarah, no! Never that. We'll re-film that scene as it was meant to be, and I promise you no one will ever see today's filming.'

'You saw it,' Sarah said bitterly. 'What will you do with it? Destroy it?'

The look she saw in his eyes made her shudder with sickness. 'You won't destroy it?' she whispered incredulously. 'You'll keep it. You'd do that to me, knowing ...'

His hand curled round her jaw, forcing her face upwards. 'Knowing what, Sarah?' he asked softly. 'That all that you feel for me is irrevocably shown on that piece of film?'

Reaction jolted through her, her inarticulate protest as she fought against the prison of his arms lost against the thickness of his robe as she tried to break free, withdrawing like a child in pain when her hand inadvertently touched his skin.

'Would you like to see it?'

'No!' Her cry was pure terror, and she felt herself falling into blackness, falling, falling until there was nothing but a deep pit of terror.

Some time later she woke and was handed a glass, a smiling but firm uniformed nurse urging her to drink. The fear that her mind had actually gone and she was indeed in some institution began to haunt her, although she was dimly aware that the room she was in was one she recognised and the nurse had been concerned rather than constraining.

The next time she opened her eyes, the sun was shining. Her body felt strangely weightless beneath the bedclothes and when she turned her head there was a stranger standing beside the bed smiling at her encouragingly.

'Ah, so you're back with us. You're to be congratulated, my dear, on your recuperative powers.'

'Where . . .?' Where am I? she had been about to croak, but she knew where she was, recognising her surroundings. She was in Ben's room, in Ben's bed, although she didn't remember it filled with these exotic flowers.

'You've had a nasty shock to the system,' her dark-suited companion told her, 'but it's all over now.' He was studying her so calmly and professionally that Sarah knew intuitively what he was. 'You're—you're a doctor?' She moistened her dry lips. 'Did . . . did Ben . . .'

'Yes, to both questions,' he agreed, smiling. 'You've given us all a very bad scare, young lady,' he told her mock-severely, 'especially your husband. I did think at one time you would have to be removed to hospital, but Ben was most adamant. He didn't want you waking up to find yourself in strange surroundings.'

A dim memory of endless nightmares when she had pleaded not to be committed to a mental hospital, crying that she was not insane, pleated a frown across her forehead, as she wondered how Ben could have known of those night terrors.

'What—what exactly happened to me?' she asked huskily, trying to banish her strange languor. 'I remember falling in the pool.' She remembered more than that, but she didn't want to think about it, much less talk about it.

'As you say, you fell in the pool; a not entirely unusual occurrence and certainly not one which would normally provoke the type of blackout you later suffered, but the shock coupled with the strain your husband tells me you've been under made your reaction far more severe than was expected. You're quite recovered,' he assured her with a kind smile. 'My dear, you must accept that sometimes we humans drive our minds and bodies further than they are prepared to go, and when that happens they're apt to make their objections known. Yours merely chose a particularly forceful way of doing so. You'll still feel weak for quite some time,' he told her, straightening up from the bed. 'I've told your husband that you mustn't even think of working for at least six months, if indeed you ever return to acting.' He paused and looked sombre. 'My dear, I am only telling you what you must in your heart of hearts already know. Your temperament is not such that it can absorb the intense emotions you demand of it without some degree of pain. I should think very carefully about the future . . .'

In other words she might as well make up her mind that she would never be able to return to acting, Sarah thought bitterly when she was alone. She didn't need the doctor's carefully guarded conversation to tell her how close she had come to some sort of breakdown, not entirely brought on by the agony of her love scene; not if she was honest with herself. The strain of keeping her feelings from Ben had exacerbated the situation. She sighed, tensing as the door opened to admit the subject of her thoughts, his face unexpectedly grim. He seemed to have lost weight, his tan less golden than it had been, weariness lying at the back of the green glance that searched her, and then she realised, biting hard on her lip. No more acting for six months, the doctor had told her, which meant Ben would not be able to change the end of the film.

'Doctor Lazelles tells me you're much recovered.'

'Yes.' How awkward and stilted she sounded!

'I'm sorry to have been such a nuisance. But now
... Ben, we have to talk ...' She bowed her head,
not knowing how much Doctor Lazelles had said
to him.

'Later.' Why was his voice so harsh, the planes of
his face sharply drawn and the skin stretched tight?
'This evening,' he amended huskily. 'After dinner.'

'I can get up?'

Her eagerness brought a brief smile to the
corners of his mouth, but his negative headshake
was firm. 'I'm afraid not, though ...' he was
watching her carefully, '... though I could have
dinner in here with you, I'm sure Doctor Lazelles
wouldn't object to that, if that's what you want?'

Sarah's heart started to beat heavily, her mind
trying hazily to grasp why the thought of their
having dinner together in this room should be so
much more intimate than sharing their meal in the
dining room.

'Yes, yes, that would be ... nice,' she managed
shakily, wondering wryly at her inadequate choice
of words and then shrinking back against her
pillows as Ben approached the bed.

'Sarah?' His voice questioned her withdrawal,
his eyes darkening as they surveyed her flushed
face and downcast lashes. 'I wasn't going to touch
you,' he said grimly at last. 'I only wanted to ask if
there was anything I could get you.'

He was gone before she was forced to contradict
him and tell him that her withdrawal had been
from herself and her own needs rather than any
fear of him.

She slept, and woke to find Margarita in the
room, pulling two chairs up to a small table she

had set by the window. 'You're awake.' She smiled
warmly at Sarah. 'And getting better. Now
perhaps Ben will not spend all night working in his
study, and sleeping there instead of here, in his
room. He has been like a man demented. All these
flowers . . .' She smiled again and shrugged. 'But
then that is a man in love for you. Would you like
any help?' Sarah shook her head, only realising
when Margarita had gone that she did want a bath
and that it might have been sensible to have
Margarita on hand in view of the fact that she
hadn't been out of bed for nearly a week. The
truth of this suspicion was proved when she swung
her feet to the floor and tried to take her first step,
the floor coming up towards her at an alarming
rate, although she didn't pass out, and she was just
making another attempt when the door on to the
balcony opened smoothly and Ben walked in, his
mouth compressing when he saw what she was
trying to do.

'I wanted a bath, and I never thought until
Margarita had gone,' Sarah protested, reading the
disapproval of his unspoken thoughts.

'I'll help you.'

Why did he insist on holding her like this when
he must be able to guess what it did to her? Sarah
wondered weakly as molten fire spread through
her veins, her hands automatically clutching at
Ben's shoulders as he bent to take her weight.
Inside the bathroom he sat her on a chair as
carefully as though she were made of brittle glass,
quickly running her bath even though she
protested that she could manage.

'I'll wait outside, but don't lock the door,' he

warned her as he stood up, 'and if you feel the slightest bit faint, just holler.'

The caress of the water against her skin felt like smooth silk. Her illness had drained her of energy and Sarah found it took twice as long to do everything as it had done. Consequently she had barely finished washing when the bathroom door burst open and Ben strode in, his face tight with anxiety, his body stilling as he turned and saw her just about to step out of the bath.

For one heart-wrenching moment Sarah could only stare at him, hot colour suddenly running up under her skin as she remembered her nudity, her breath caught in a gasp as Ben lifted her bodily out of the water, uncaring of her protests that she would soak his clothes, holding her pinned against him with one hand while the other reached for a towel that reached from her neck to her ankles as he strode into the bedroom with her.

While she had been in the bathroom dusk had fallen, an electric dinner waggon mute evidence that Margarita had been in with their meal. The rough movement of Ben's hands over her back, rubbing it dry, was unbearably erotic, her breasts rasped by the crisp body hair darkening his chest where his shirt had come undone. When he sat down, pulling her on to his knees, Sarah's skin flushed to think of his eyes resting on the aroused peaks of her breasts, but he barely glanced at her body as he secured the towel firmly round her, oblivious to his own damp shirt clinging slickly to his skin where her body had pressed against it.

'Ben, there's something I have to tell you.' She

felt him tense as she spoke, his eyes as green and wary as a big cat's.

'When Doctor Lazelles was here he said . . . He said I mustn't think of returning to filming for at least six months.' She couldn't look at him, knowing what her admission would mean.

'And you're worried about your career? You needn't be,' he said lightly. 'With my fifty per cent interest in the studio I'm sure I can get my wife some work . . .'

Sarah shook her head. 'No, you don't understand. I'm not sure if I'll ever act again, so I'm not concerned about future roles, but *Richard*, Ben, my . . . my love scene . . .' Her voice trembled and threatened to desert her. She couldn't bring herself to look at him and hoped he wouldn't see how much she was trembling.

'I told you not to worry about that, Sarah. It won't ever be shown, I promise you, and if I can't destroy it—well, you'll have to put that down to . . .'

'But you'll have to show it! Don't you see? If I can't work for six months you'll either have to re-film completely using someone else, or use that scene. You can't delay completion . . .'

'Who says I can't?' Ben drawled arrogantly, adding huskily, 'Sarah, if I thought it would atone for the pain I've caused you I'd cheerfully consign the whole damn film to the flames. Have you any conception what it did to me standing by that bed listening to you begging me to rescue you from a mental hospital? Dear God, and you thought *you* were going off your head! It's nothing to what I felt. And anyway, I wouldn't use that scene. I couldn't. When I saw the rushes and saw the look on your face when I made love to you, I knew there was no way I was going to share that with anyone else in the world, and I was only amazed that I hadn't seen it for myself at the time. My only excuse is that I was raw inside with hurting and jealousy. Wanting you ... loving you ... hating Dale, as I'd always hated him for taking you from me. You'll never know how many times in these last years I've nearly been on that plane to come and get you, only to tell myself that it wasn't fair to you; that you didn't love me, and that the only reason you'd married me was that I'd bullied you into it, and because I'd taken your virginity. Dale lied to you, Sarah,' he said slowly, 'there never was any bet. It's true that I meant to have you right from the first, but as my wife ... nothing else. Can you try and believe that?'

'You love me?' Sarah could hardly believe it. Beneath the protective towel she shivered convulsively, her eyes darkening in awed amazement.

'If you don't believe me I'll show you the film. It does more than merely show your feelings, Sarah. If a man's body can tell a woman that he aches and yearns for her, mine did.'

'But you were always so angry ... so ...'

'With myself for still loving you, for not being able to *stop* loving you. God, I damn nearly wanted to kill Paul simply for kissing you, and that was in the script!'

Sarah laughed huskily, remembering Eva's comment that he was jealous. Then she hadn't believed her, but now ...

'After *Richard* I'm not doing any more

directing,' Ben told her. 'I want to concentrate on writing, but we won't be paupers, I've still got my interest in the studio, or am I going ahead too fast? Will you stay with me, Sarah, live with me; love me; bear my children? You know, Dale made one big mistake,' he told her quietly. 'He thought because I'd made you do that scene that I no longer loved you, and so he told me everything. What he didn't realise was that I was punishing myself, forcing myself to endure watching you in someone else's arms, telling myself it was either kill or cure.'

'And then you had to take Paul's place.'

'And I saw in your face how much you dreaded the thought of me doing so and saw red . . .'

'Because I knew I wouldn't be able to resist you,' Sarah said dreamily.

'And does that still hold good now?' The teasing quality had gone from Ben's voice, his face strained and vulnerable. Sarah let her fingertips explore the newly sharpened angles, realising with a pang that they were there on her account.

'For God's sake, Sarah,' he muttered thickly, grasping her wrist and turning his mouth into her palm. 'Don't toy with me, even though I know I deserve it. You haven't answered my question. Do you still love me?'

'So much,' Sarah admitted shakily. 'So very, very much!'

The pressure of his lips was no longer that of a supplicant, but Sarah didn't object, not even when his hands pushed aside her towel to study the pale curves of her body, her movements deliberately teasing as she stretched provocatively beneath his glance, yawning against her hand, claiming that she felt tired.

'You're no actress, my lady,' Ben muttered thickly against her ear, 'and as your director I ought to beat you for that hopeless performance—as it is I think I shall merely have to punish you by accepting the invitation this . . .' and he ran his hands slowly over her body, '. . . has just proffered. Unless of course you've any objections?'

'None, unless it be your tardiness, my lord,' Sarah drawled languidly, matching his mood, watching the little flames of green burn within his eyes, boneless and sensual as a small cat as her skin luxuriated in his touch, her ears filled by the sound of his murmured love words, feeling her body quicken in sexual excitement, Margarita's dinner forgotten as the shadows of dusk gave way to darkness and she finally rested in the sanctuary of her husband's arms.

A WORD ABOUT THE AUTHOR

Born in Preston, a small city north of Liverpool, England, Penny Jordan was constantly in trouble as a schoolgirl because of her inability to stop daydreaming—the first sign of possible talent as a writer! When she was not daydreaming, she spent most of her spare time curled up somewhere with a book. Early in her teens she was introduced to romance novels and became an avid reader, but at the time it didn't occur to her to try to write one herself.

That changed when she entered her thirties and felt an urge to make a mark in the world by means of her own talent. She had many false starts—lots of "great" ideas ended up in the wastepaper basket. But finally the day came when Penny completed her first book-length manuscript. And, to her utter amazement, it wasn't long before the novel was accepted for publication.

Now she has received many letters of acceptance for her books, and every letter brings the thrill of knowing that the stories on which she has worked so hard will reach the readers for whom each is lovingly written.

Coming Next Month in Harlequin Presents!

Harlequin Photo ~ Calendar ~

Turn Your Favorite Photo into a Calendar.

JULY 1984

The Browns

Uniquely yours, this 10x17½" calendar features your favorite photograph, with any name you wish in attractive lettering at the bottom. A delightfully personal and practical idea!

Send us your favorite color print, black-and-white print, negative, or slide, any size (we'll return it), along with 3 proofs of purchase (coupon below) from a June or July release of Harlequin Romance, Harlequin Presents, Harlequin Superromance, Harlequin American Romance or Harlequin Temptation, plus $5.75 (includes shipping and handling).

Harlequin Photo Calendar Offer
(PROOF OF PURCHASE)

NAME_____

(Please Print)

ADDRESS_____

CITY_____ STATE_____ ZIP_____

NAME ON CALENDAR_____

Mail photo, 3 proofs,
plus check or money order
for $5.75 payable to:

Harlequin Books
P.O. Box 52020
Phoenix, AZ 85072

2-2

Offer expires December 31, 1984. (Not available in Canada)

CAL-1